THE MISCHIEVOUS MISS CHARLOTTE

SCHOOL OF CHARM

MAGGIE DALLEN

CHAPTER ONE

The armoire in Miss Charlotte's room at the young ladies' finishing school was surprisingly spacious.

Charlotte shifted against the billowing skirts of one ball-gown and the silk bodice of another. Her spectacles fogged over as her own hot air filled the small space.

Drawing in a deep breath, she tried to make herself comfortable, but the air was growing thicker and more cloying by the moment.

As Charlotte had only just arrived at London's esteemed School of Charm, her maid hadn't even finished unpacking her trunks. So indeed, the wardrobe *was* surprisingly spacious.

But it was still a wardrobe, and hence, not *that* spacious.

Definitely not meant to hold a grown lady such as herself. She fidgeted as her leg cramped. As a child, armoires like this one had made for a much more pleasant hiding spot.

Her skin prickled with uncomfortable heat as she waited for the seconds to pass. Her back was beginning to ache. She tried to shift for a better position, but the movement sent dust flying and her nose crinkled as she fought a sneeze.

Surely Lord Thomas and his mother would not wait for long if she could not be found.

But then, if there was one thing she knew of the Earl of Calloway's family, it was that they were persistent. Painfully so.

She'd hoped that with her years away on the continent, traveling as a companion to her elderly aunt, the earl and his wife might have lost patience and done away with the understanding that had been agreed upon when she was still in the nursery.

Indeed, she'd optimistically assumed everyone had forgotten that small matter of her impending marriage to the earl's younger son.

But that had not been the case. The very first words her mother had greeted her with when she'd stepped foot on English soil were, "At last we can make your engagement official and get this wedding underway."

There had been hugs and kisses as well, of course, from her brother and her sister. But those very first words of welcome had dashed her hopes that the understanding had been forgotten. Needless to say, it had not been the warm welcome of Charlotte's dreams.

In fact, it had been more like a scene from one of her more horrific nightmares. She'd said as much to her sister, but Eloise had declared her protests histrionic.

But then, Eloise had never minded her own arranged engagement, and so she could not possibly understand. She even claimed to get on quite well with her fiancé, Lord Pickington, the old bore. Never mind the fact that she'd have to answer to the name Lady Pickington for the rest of her life.

So no, of course Eloise hadn't understood her fears.

I've met your intended, Eloise had said in that haughty way of hers. *He's an excellent choice for you.*

Which, coming from Eloise, only made Charlotte more

frightened. For Eloise, like Mother, believed the best thing for Charlotte was to find a man who'd take her in hand and finally succeed in making her the obedient and dutiful young lady they wished her to be.

Charlotte clasped her hands together and willed herself not to sneeze.

They'd be gone any moment now, and then she could disentangle herself from her gowns and pretend she had not heard her visitors arrive.

She could avoid the inevitable for one day longer, at least. Her head fell back against the wood panel of the armoire with a thud. Was it her imagination or could she actually hear the bells tolling for her demise?

All right, yes. Perhaps Eloise had a point about her tendency for histrionics. Lord Thomas was likely not the evil villain she feared him to be. But he was still a stranger. She'd never met the man, though she'd heard about him. Sweet heavens, how much she'd heard.

Her mother's letters were filled with mentions of the man, only two years older than Charlotte but, by the sounds of it, with the demeanor of an old man. *Just like his father,* her mother had written. *What good manners. Such noble bearing. Stern, quiet, proper, et cetera.*

It didn't take much to decipher that he was a stodgy, unbearable, pretentious bore.

Quite a leap you're making there, her Great Aunt Ida had said. But it wasn't. Because Charlotte might not have met Lord Thomas, but she had met his father on occasion and to say he was a stodgy, pretentious bore would be a kind understatement.

She heard a female voice coming from the hallway. No doubt the new headmistress, Miss Farthington, calling out for her.

Miss Farthington likely thought she'd be ecstatic that her

soon-to-be fiancé had called on her on her first day in town. But Miss Farthington would be wrong.

It was nerves and not heat that had a bead of sweat forming on her brow. *Oh please don't let them find me.*

Another female voice joined the mix, and Charlotte tensed as both voices grew closer.

They were in her bedroom.

Charlotte held her breath.

"Have you seen her, Miss Mary?" Miss Farthington's voice said.

"She was here a moment ago," Miss Mary said.

Charlotte and Mary were both new to the school. Miss Farthington too, for that matter. The school had been formed by the Earl of Charmian—better known as the Earl of Charm—as a present of sorts for his wife. Apparently, she was fond of helping young ladies acquire the appropriate skills to make them pillars of good society. Though, busy as Lady Charmian was as a countess, she had little to do with the day-to-day running of the school.

Instead, they'd hired a Miss Grayson originally to help teach young ladies the social graces they'd need upon entering society. Miss Grayson had done such a wonderful job of it that every young lady in her charge had married and married well. Even Miss Grayson had found a marquess for a husband, which was how Miss Farthington had come to take her place.

With such wonderful matches made during its first year of existence, the School of Charm was quite in demand for all the young ladies of the *ton* who were either still in need of a match or lacked the necessary traits needed to be the ideal wife in the eyes of the *ton*.

As it had been understood that Charlotte would marry Lord Thomas when she came of age, she obviously fell in the latter category. But as she listened to Miss Mary Evermoor converse with Miss Farthington on the other side of the wardrobe door, she wondered what had brought *her* to this school.

Perhaps they might one day be close enough that she could ask.

Charlotte had been on her best behavior the first time they'd met, and if she could only manage to keep her nose out of trouble, perhaps Miss Mary and Miss Farthington would think well of her, and she'd finally have friends who—

"Achoo!" Charlotte's sneeze came on quite unexpectedly.

It was also excessively loud.

The silence on the other side of the wardrobe doors was telling, and Miss Charlotte was still wincing when the doors to the armoire were thrown open.

She found herself blinking at the sudden light and the two pretty-yet-stricken faces which greeted her.

Miss Farthington recovered first. "Miss Charlotte," she said.

That was all. But it was enough. The question underlying her words was clear indeed.

"Er, yes," Charlotte said as she went to climb out of the wardrobe.

Miss Mary quickly stepped forward and offered a hand, her gaze no longer shocked but rather filled with amusement. Charlotte decided right then and there that she and Mary would be friends. For her lack of derision alone, Charlotte liked her immensely.

"I was just...checking, you see," Charlotte said, her voice too breathy and high as she swiped errant, wispy blonde curls from her face.

The wardrobe had wreaked havoc on the chignon her maid had done for her, but she tried her best to correct it as she faced the petite brunette who now ran this school.

Her expression was hard to read, but Charlotte saw her lips twitching.

With anger?

Charlotte pressed her lips together and bit the inside of her cheek. Oh drat. Now she'd gone and made a bad name for herself on her very first day at this school.

"You were...checking?" Miss Farthington repeated. Her gaze moved beyond Charlotte to the wardrobe beyond. "Making sure all of your gowns will fit, I imagine."

Charlotte's lips parted with a gape. Miss Farthington's voice was mild but there was that twitch of her lips again.

Was it disdain or was it...laughter?

No, it couldn't be amusement. Charlotte didn't know Miss Farthington well, but she'd heard the rumors. The daughter of a viscount, her reputation had taken a bit of a ding after her long-standing engagement came to an end for reasons no one knew for certain—though nearly everyone seemed to have a suspicion.

It was how she'd come to be here, running a finishing school rather than out in society with a beau of her own.

Miss Farthington and Miss Mary seemed to be waiting for her to speak. To explain. Charlotte drew in a deep breath. "Yes, Miss Farthington," she said with as much pride as she could muster. "I wanted to ensure there would be enough space for the costume I brought along for the upcoming masquerade."

Miss Mary was staring wide-eyed, disbelief and amusement making her dark eyes sparkle and her round cheeks pinken. No doubt on Charlotte's behalf.

Charlotte's sweet older sister used to blush for her too, though it was rarely tempered with amusement. Just embarrassment on her behalf, plain and simple.

Another point in Miss Mary's favor. Empathy was such a lovely quality in a friend.

"Well, I don't suppose you heard their arrival," Miss Farthington managed with a straight face. "But you have visitors."

"Do I?" Charlotte was certain her attempt at shock fooled no one, yet everyone seemed to have come to a silent agreement that they would see this charade through to the end.

"Indeed," Miss Farthington said, her lips still twitching.

"Whoever might it be?" Charlotte asked. Perhaps she was taking it a bit too far.

"Lady Calloway and her son, Lord Thomas," Miss Farthington continued. "They are in the drawing room at the moment."

Charlotte's stomach sank to her toes. "Are they?"

Her forced smile faltered. Drat. There was no escape.

She'd have to meet him one day or another, she told herself. It might as well be today.

With a deep breath, Charlotte pushed her shoulders back and lifted her chin. But before she could say *oh, all right, let's get this over with,* Miss Farthington continued. "But I suppose I shall have to send them away."

Miss Charlotte blinked and Miss Mary turned to give the headmistress a curious look.

"You're clearly not well," Miss Farthington said.

Charlotte stared at her. She wasn't?

"Oh yes, you're quite right, Miss Farthington," Miss Mary said, her lips curving up in a smile that made her go from plain to beautiful so quickly, Charlotte blinked in surprise. "That sneeze just now," Miss Mary added, her eyes widening and her brows arched as if she were prompting Charlotte.

"Oh!" Charlotte's head snapped up as she understood what they were doing. "That's right. I am a bit under the weather."

Miss Farthington nodded. "Just as I thought." She turned

to leave. "I'll tell Lady Calloway and her son that they'd do well to try again on another day."

Charlotte's shoulders slumped with relief. "Thank you, Miss Farthington."

Miss Farthington's response was a wink, so quick and sly it made Charlotte laugh out loud in surprise as the headmistress disappeared.

Miss Mary's head tipped to the side as they found themselves alone. "Would you care to tell me what that was about, or shall I pretend that nothing is amiss?"

Charlotte smiled with true delight at the question. "I do so love young ladies who get straight to the point." She moved past Mary to sit on the edge of her bed. "And I suppose I do owe you an explanation."

Mary shrugged. "Only if you wish to share."

Just like that. As if she was not judging one way or the other.

Oh yes, she and Mary would most definitely be friends.

"Well, you see—" She cut herself off as the sound of voices in the entryway carried upstairs.

A young man's low rumble and an older woman's higher pitch. Charlotte swallowed hard, unease slithering in her veins. She couldn't avoid him forever, and it wasn't like her to be such a coward.

Just a few days, she promised herself. She needed time to reacquaint herself with England and London society first, that was all. Then she would face the inevitable.

"You do not enjoy the company of Lady Calloway, is that it?" Mary asked.

Charlotte's eyes widened in surprise. There was forthright and then there was Mary, it seemed. "Er, something like that."

Mary arched a brow. "Or perhaps it is Lord Thomas you do not wish to see."

Charlotte let out a huff of amusement. "You are quite persistent, aren't you?"

Mary's grin was unapologetic. "That is one word for it. Not the one my family uses, but I prefer persistent."

Charlotte laughed. "I don't particularly enjoy the words my family uses to describe me, either."

Mary leaned forward, her eyes sparkling with laughter. "I suppose that's why we are both here."

Charlotte let her head tip back with a laugh. "They're trying to keep you out of trouble too?"

Mary pursed her lips as she considered that. "More like, they're trying to soften my harder edges." She shrugged. "Also, they're keeping me out of sight until my sister makes a good match. They wouldn't want me getting in the way of that, and I wouldn't wish to either."

Charlotte nodded, but her heart went out to the other woman. She knew all too well what it was like to be shuffled off and kept out of sight. "My sister already made a match, although the wedding is not for another few months. I'm to be next, you see."

"Ah." Mary tilted her head toward the bedroom door. "And Lord Thomas is one of your prospective suitors?"

"More like, he is my *expected* suitor," she said. "Our parents have an understanding."

"But you don't like him," Mary guessed.

"I've never met him," Charlotte admitted. "I was a little too troublesome for my family, particularly when my parents were trying to find a husband for my sister Eloise and my brother was just coming into his own. And besides, my great aunt truly did need a companion these past few years." She sounded too defensive, even to her own ears, but Mary's gaze was nothing but understanding.

Then again, Mary was also here, living at a finishing school rather than her own home. She likely *did* understand.

"So you were allowed to travel the continent?" Mary's eyes were wide and excited. "How lovely."

"It was, rather." Charlotte smiled as happy memories came back to her. "My great aunt did not have enough energy to see all that I'd hoped, but I did a great deal more than most young ladies, and I appreciated every second of it."

"Oh, I should love to hear about your travels," Mary said with a wistful sigh. "I never get to go anywhere. Most of my life was spent at my family's country estate." She wrinkled her nose. "I feel out of place even here in London. I couldn't imagine being in a foreign land where no one spoke the same language."

"It was heaven," Charlotte admitted with a sigh. It was far more enjoyable to seem strange in a foreign land than to be a stranger in one's own family. She hadn't been back in England for long, but long enough to know that she still did not fit in here any better now than she had two years ago when she'd left. Oh, her older brother Rodrick had been happy to see her. Eloise, too. But the fact that her parents had immediately shipped her off to this finishing school made it apparent that no matter how much time she'd spent away—it hadn't been enough.

But with Aunt Ida, she'd never had to worry about fitting in. For Ida was eccentric. *A boon of getting old,* her great aunt would say with a cackle. *You can say or do anything you want and no one cares.*

Charlotte envied her. Part of her wished she could be an old spinster of independent means like Ida, but that would never happen so long as her parents and Lord Thomas had anything to say about it.

"If you've never met Lord Thomas, how do you know you won't like him?" Mary asked.

Charlotte turned to look at her new friend. "I don't have

to meet him to know." She took a deep breath. "I've met his father."

Mary stared. Then she blinked. Finally, she breathed, "Heavens."

"Indeed."

Mary's lips quirked. "I do not know how you managed to make that simple phrase sound so fearsome, but I got chills."

Charlotte laughed. "I cannot exaggerate just how intimidating the earl can be. He's overbearing and so dreadfully serious." She feigned a shudder. "And everyone who knows Lord Thomas keeps telling me just how alike they are."

"I see," Mary said with a grimace. "That is unfortunate."

Charlotte's sigh was admittedly dramatic. "Quite so."

After a moment, when it was clear by the silence from below that the threat was gone, Mary turned to her with arched brows. "I was planning on going shopping today. Would it cheer you to accompany me?"

Charlotte winced. "For ribbons and the like?"

That was what her sister was forever seeking out. As if browsing fabrics and fripperies gave her purpose in life.

Mary winced. "Oh heavens no. For books."

Charlotte leapt up from the bed with excitement. "A bookshop? Of course, I'll join you. On the way there, you must tell me what sort of literature you like to read."

"Oh, no literature," Mary said. "I prefer science. And maths."

Her cheeks turned pink again, and Charlotte laughed. "You truly are a treasure, aren't you?"

Mary shrugged as they headed out toward the hallway. "If so, you'd be the first to say so."

"Well, I'm certain I won't be the last," Charlotte said as she linked arms with her friend, and they headed for the spiral staircase. "You are bound to make loads of friends here in London."

"Miss Farthington says we're expecting more young ladies over the next few weeks," Mary said. "I hope they're all as easy to get along with as you are."

Charlotte let out a little snort of amusement. "Easy to get along with, you think? I shall have to tell my family."

"They don't believe you're friendly?"

"Friendly? Yes. Perhaps too much so. In fact, according to my mother I'm too much of just about everything. Too loud, too quick to laugh, too mawkish, too romantic." She grinned without remorse. "You name it, and I'm too much of it."

Mary giggled. "Well, not everyone enjoys my candid way of speaking so much as you seem to."

"Oh I do enjoy it," Charlotte said, coming to her feet and feeling a whole lot lighter now than she had all day. "It makes talking so much easier when I don't have to talk around the topic. Don't you think so, Miss Mary?"

"That's what I say," Mary exclaimed with wide eyes. "And do please call me Mary."

Charlotte leaned into her new friend. "Then you must call me Lottie. All my dear friends do."

This was not necessarily true. It was what her brother, sister, and Great Aunt Ida called her, but were she to have any dear friends, she deduced that this was what they would call her as well.

"Lottie," Mary said with a smile that warmed Charlotte's heart.

"Do you know, Mary..." Charlotte leaned forward and lowered her voice. "I think we shall be very good friends."

Mary beamed. "I think so too, Lottie."

CHAPTER TWO

Thomas's friend was watching him warily as they strolled down the street toward the bookstore.

"What's wrong with you?" Lord Paul asked. Likely because he was smiling. For no apparent reason.

Thomas wasn't often known to smile—not even when he had reason.

But now? Well, now Thomas grinned, tipping his head back to take in the sunshine. "Just enjoying this glorious day, my friend. Is that so wrong?"

Snow melting from the trees overhead dripped onto his nose, belying the 'glorious day' sentiment.

"Hmph." His friend made a show of peering at him with unbridled suspicion. "Last I heard, you were meant to be accompanying your mother to visit your fiancée—"

"Not my fiancée yet," Thomas pointed out, his smile growing.

Paul stopped walking to turn and face him. "Right." His dark brows furrowed and he rocked back on his heels. "I suppose all your concerns were unfounded then, eh? Was she better than you'd expected?"

Thomas's smile faltered. She was likely worse than he expected, if his mother's descriptions were anything to go by. *Just like her mother,* she'd said.

Which was truly a shame because Thomas had met her mother.

Fashionable? Yes. But that was where his complimentary descriptions of her mother began and ended.

"Ah," Paul said, a smirk on his lips as he assessed Thomas. "I believe I understand."

Thomas cleared his throat. "I didn't actually meet her. Yet," he added quickly.

Because he would. Of course, he would. He couldn't put this off forever, and heaven knew his parents wouldn't let him even if he wished to. It seemed both families had much to gain by this union, and no amount of pleading for mercy had ever done him any good.

When it came to this arrangement, his father was particularly inflexible. As the spare to the heir, his marrying well was all that was expected of him, as his father so kindly pointed out.

"Miss Charlotte wasn't in for visitors?" Paul asked.

"She was indisposed." Thomas's lip curled at the word.

His mind filled with an image of her mother with her smelling salts. The last time she'd come to visit she'd swooned no less than three times, and each instance required several servants to wait on her hand and foot before she was deemed well enough to return to a strenuous afternoon of cards and gossip.

Thomas felt a headache starting at the mere thought of being married to a woman who was anything like Lady Meagher.

"So you're just pleased because you've been granted a reprieve," Paul said with a laugh.

Thomas shrugged. Let his friend laugh. He'd take whatever freedom he could get until his bachelor days were over.

Not that he was living it up as a bachelor, necessarily. Paul had embraced the role of the eligible, rakish gentleman far more than Thomas had after their school days. And even now, it was Paul who enjoyed the balls, soirees, and outings.

Unlike Thomas, Paul was a flirt through and through.

In fact, in most ways Thomas was the exact opposite of his old chum. Their friendship had begun at school when they'd realized they were both second sons. Forgotten ones at that. After spending a few holidays alone at school together while their families traveled without them, they'd become close friends.

Nearly brothers.

But being spares was really all they had in common. Where Paul had dark hair, Thomas's was a light brown. Nearly blond in certain lights. And while Paul had a rugged demeanor and enjoyed all sorts of sportsmanship, Thomas far preferred books.

Paul was outgoing while Thomas enjoyed solitude, and where Paul had no love of the arts, Thomas hated to miss any new exhibit.

Though miss them, he often did when his parents were in town. His father, in particular, did not appreciate Thomas's appreciation of the arts.

Paul tended to be cynical while Thomas was an admitted romantic, Paul was sought out by young ladies, whereas most everyone kept their distance from Thomas.

The list went on and on, but they'd agreed long ago that it was their differences that made them such excellent friends. Not because they agreed on everything—or even anything, for that matter. But they tended to complement one another. Each filled in the gaps where the other was lacking.

And right now, Paul seemed to believe that Thomas was lacking in sense.

"You know you cannot avoid her forever, don't you?" Paul asked.

Thomas glanced over at his friend. He refused to let anything get him down today. He had one more afternoon to pretend that his future was his and his life might be a happy one. He wasn't about to let Paul ruin that.

But Paul was being a little too grumpy for even Paul's standards.

"Everything all right, mate?" Thomas asked.

Paul scoffed. "Fine. Just dandy."

Thomas winced at his friend's sarcasm. "Are you going to tell me what's wrong or shall I beat it out of you at Jack's?"

Paul's lips curved up in a grudging grin. "I'd like to see you try."

Paul was most definitely the better pugilist.

But Thomas was the better at keeping silent. Patience was far more his virtue than Paul's, so he opted to wait him out.

Thomas arched his brows and turned forward in the direction they'd been heading. They were on their way to a gentlemen's club, but Paul needed to stop to pick up a book he'd ordered for his mother.

Thomas had offered to accompany him. And why not on such a glorious day as this? The snow was melting, the sun was shining, and birds were chirping in the trees.

And oh yes. He'd avoided an encounter which would surely mark the beginning of the end of his happiness.

His days of solitude would be behind him for good. As it was, he had to contend with his father's urgings for him to join him hunting or drinking and gambling with his friends. Time to himself was a rare gift.

Now those precious few moments when he could enjoy pastimes of his own choosing...well, they'd be eaten up by all the countless activities his new wife would want him to participate in. Even his meals would be spent trying to conjure polite small talk or feigned interest in ribbons or gowns or whatever it was women talked about when they were alone.

He shuddered at the thought.

Right. He was supposed to be focusing on enjoying the moment, not counting down to his own demise. He steadfastly focused on the little flashes of green in the trees and shrubberies that lined the sidewalk, the telltale signs that spring was on its way. Paul finally lost the battle with patience as Thomas knew he would.

"All right, fine," Paul burst out eventually. "My father is forcing me to wed."

Thomas turned to his friend in alarm. They both knew that eventually this day would come—they might not be heirs, but they still had a responsibility to the family. Connections and fortunes were always at stake, it seemed.

But Paul's father was more tolerant than Thomas's parents, and Paul had always enjoyed far more freedom.

"Who?" Thomas asked.

Paul shrugged. "Don't know."

Thomas blinked. "So they haven't picked her out for you?"

Lucky bloke.

"Not *yet*," Paul said, his tone grim.

Thomas turned to face his friend. "Would they?"

Paul shrugged again, but his scowl spoke of despair. "They could."

"Then you'd best start courting someone of your choosing," Thomas said.

Paul shot him a glare, but Thomas ignored it. He was hard-pressed to feel too sorry for his friend. They all had to marry eventually. And there were times Thomas even liked the thought of a wife and children. A family of his own in a home filled with happiness and warmth.

But then he'd remember Lady Meagher and her megrims and he dismissed all such notions as utter nonsense.

"Start courting?" Paul echoed, disbelief in his tone. "You make it sound so simple."

"For you it is," he shot back.

Paul could still have his pick of a wife. He was a charmer with the ladies when he wished to be, and with those gentlemanly qualities that made him a desirable son-in-law in the eyes of parents.

"You must have met every eligible lady of the *ton* by now," Thomas said. "Pick the one you like best, that's all."

"That's all," Paul repeated with a mocking edge. "And all you have to do is marry the Meagher chit. *That's all.*" His voice was all out taunting, though he softened it with a laugh.

Thomas shrugged. "All I'm saying is, we both have to marry at some point. I'd far prefer your freedom to choose than my lot." He glanced over. "Wouldn't you?"

His friend grunted. "Don't know," he muttered. "I've never met your intended." He leaned over to give Thomas a shove that had him stumbling. "And neither have you."

"Yes, yes. I know. I'll meet her soon enough, and then—oy!" He shouted in surprise when Paul shoved him again, but this time into the blasted shrubberies beside him. "What was that for?"

Paul grimaced, his gaze fixed straight ahead. "I don't think she saw me."

Thomas blinked and followed his gaze just in time to see a skirt disappear into the bookstore. "Who?"

"A nasty little termagant from my youth," he muttered.

Thomas arched his brows, and when Paul glanced over he was smirking. "Trust me, it's better if Mary and I don't meet."

"She's that awful?"

Paul's smirk faltered. "She despises me that much."

"For what?"

Paul threw his hands up. "How should I know? We were children when our little feud started. I don't even know what she's doing here, to tell you the truth. I thought she never left their country estate."

Thomas opened his mouth to ask questions. He had many on the tip of his tongue. But Paul was shoving him again, this time in the direction of the bookshop. "Be a sport and go fetch that book for me, won't you?"

It wasn't really a request. More like a command. Especially with the pushing.

"Are you really so scared of a girl?" Thomas couldn't help a laugh.

His friend glared at him. "You'd be scared too if you knew Mary."

Thomas laughed harder now. He'd never known his friend to avoid a lady. *Any* lady. He enjoyed flirting with the opposite sex as much as Thomas enjoyed his solitude. "If she's so frightening, what am I supposed to do with her?"

"Don't be daft," Paul muttered. "She won't come anywhere near you."

Thomas drew his chin back, uncertain whether he should be offended by that. "Why not?"

Paul rolled his eyes. "She'll be too intimidated by you."

Thomas stopped short, ignoring the hard shove. Paul might be bigger, but Thomas was no weakling. "No one is intimidated by me."

Paul's eyes widened in surprise. "Thomas, *everyone* is intimidated by you."

Thomas frowned.

"See?" Paul pointed to his face. "That's why, right there. Haven't you noticed how the crowds tend to part for you when we're in a crush?"

Thomas sputtered a bit. His father was intimidating, yes. Everyone knew that. He was tall, with stern features—not unlike Thomas's, now that he thought about it.

And his father was quiet, too. But that wasn't the same thing at all. He wasn't at all like his father.

Well, except for perhaps his appearance. A knot formed in his gut. He'd gone his whole life trying to please his father and watching everyone around him do the same. Surely others didn't see him that way.

He turned to Paul. "Do people truly fear me?"

Paul gave him another shove. "I'm not afraid to knock out your teeth if you don't go in there and get my book for me."

"I—"

But Paul had already opened the door and was shoving him inside. He shoved him so hard that Thomas careened into the shop—

And ran right into a young lady.

"Oh!" She whirled about, her eyes blue and wide behind her spectacles. A feather from her cap fell over her face. She batted it away as she spun, but Thomas was standing on the hem of her gown, and in one spectacular movement of flailing arms and scuffling feet, she fell.

Directly into his arms.

He held her low, her legs out in front of her and her hands clinging to his shoulders.

Beautiful.

That was his first thought as she blinked up at him.

Then she smiled and he lost the ability to think altogether.

"How do you do?" she said, polite as could be—before bursting out in a laugh that the birds outside must surely envy. It was light, and sweet, and merry, and she went from beautiful to breathtaking.

He couldn't breathe. He definitely couldn't speak.

He was never much for words, but now mere thoughts were apparently more than he could handle.

Instead, he focused on setting her to rights and helping her to unbind her skirts from around her legs. He took a step back quickly when he realized how close he was, and just how inappropriately he'd been touching her.

He glanced around the small, cluttered shop but found no one was watching. The clerk was peering down at an open ledger before him and while he could see the top of a lady's bonnet behind one of the rows of bookshelves, he and this stranger were hidden from view.

"So careless of me," she was saying, her voice still light and happy.

"No, no," he finally managed to say. "That was my fault entirely."

"Was it?" she asked. "I was so caught up in reading I was sure I must have backed up into you."

"No, no, it was my fault," he said. "I must make it up to you."

It seemed like the polite thing to say and he waited for her to protest in a similarly polite fashion. But instead she turned that smile up in his direction and her eyes fairly twinkled with mischief. "All right," she said.

He blinked. "Pardon?"

"If you wish to make it up to me, I certainly won't stop you," she continued. "I accept all manner of gifts, but I'm partial to diamonds and pearls."

"Diamonds and—" He burst out in a laugh when he realized she was teasing. He shocked himself with that laugh.

He laughed with Paul at times, but never with a young lady, and never with a stranger to whom he hadn't even been introduced.

Oh, this would not do.

She was backing away now as if she too were remembering that they had not been introduced. He didn't like to see her walking away from him.

That also would not do.

He frowned. *Stay.* That was what he wished to say. He just barely held back the short command. And thank goodness, too. She was obviously not a dog that he could bark orders at like that. She was a beautiful young lady, clearly gently bred and deserving of the utmost respect.

Stay. Too bad his mind had chosen this moment to turn to dust. He couldn't think of any eloquent words when she smiled at him so.

She was enchanting. Everything about her, from the silly feather in her cap to the pale-yellow gown, to the slippers on her feet.

She was beautiful, yes. But she also...glowed.

No, that wasn't the right word for it. She *was* radiant, though. He knew not how to explain it, but he saw it. He felt it. She buzzed with energy and her smile held more life than he'd seen in all his days.

"Lottie?" A woman called from the other side of the shop, but he couldn't see her.

"Coming!" his lady in yellow called back.

"Wait," he started. Panic set in at the thought of her leaving.

"Are you here for Lord Paul?" the shopkeeper called out. He must have recognized him from when he'd come here with his friend the last time. Thomas glanced over and the bookshop clerk arched his brows. "You're here for the books addressed to Lord Paul, yes?"

"Er, yes," he said.

The shopkeeper smiled and patted the stack. "Please do give Lady Galena our best regards."

"Yes, yes of course." Though he couldn't say when he'd be

seeing Paul's mother again. He turned back to see that his lady was...squatting.

He blinked down at her and realized belatedly that she'd dropped something during their run-in. Oh blast. Where were his manners? He rushed to bend down and help her. "Please, allow me—oof!"

He grunted when her head came up suddenly and knocked his nose.

"Oh dear," she said, her eyes wide. "How very clumsy of me."

"No, no, not at all."

Her smile was so rueful and genuine. "I suppose many ladies knock skulls with you when you're out on the town?"

"Every day," he said mildly.

He was rewarded with another tinkling laugh. "How horrible for you," she teased. "You must have a perpetual headache."

"No, just a very thick skull," he said.

She laughed.

What was he doing? What was he saying? For the first time in his life, his mouth decided to function, and he was uttering inanities.

But those inanities were making her laugh and so he would not stop. He would be the veriest fool if it meant she kept smiling at him like she was right now.

This lady wasn't intimidated, not in the least.

"I ought to get back to my friend," she said, glancing behind her. "Lord Paul, was it?"

He nodded, and then her words hit him a moment later.

A moment too late.

"It was a pleasure to meet you, Lord Paul," she said with another smile. A shy one.

It was a smile that made his heart twist and turn in his

chest as though it had been long dormant and just now stirring for the first time.

He looked down at the book in his hands and blinked in surprise. Frankenstein.

Yes. Yes, that was precisely how he felt. Like this woman and her brilliant smile had just brought him to life.

Her cheeks were pink when he glanced back up and she tucked her hands behind her back. "I truly ought to go."

"Wait, please," he said, resisting the urge to reach out to her. "Don't leave."

CHAPTER THREE

Don't leave.

Oh heavens. She couldn't have moved if she'd tried. The look in his eyes was so very arresting. Her body was quite paralyzed. But her heart...

Oh, her heart would surely give out if it kept up this frantic pace.

His eyes were a golden brown, and his features so handsome something in her belly began to flutter. Not classically handsome, but rather...frighteningly so. Her throat was too dry, and her hands trembled.

His jaw was square, his nose a straight line. There was no softness in his visage, only sharp lines and harsh features. But he was handsome nonetheless, in a way that reminded her of the ruins of Pompeii or The Parthenon in Greece. Classic. Mysterious.

Rather awe-inspiring, actually.

Which was perhaps why she was still frozen in place, gaping at him like a fool.

"My friend is calling," she said as she backed away.

She truly didn't want to leave, but in the back of her mind

she could hear her mother's voice, urging her to be good. To keep her head bowed and her voice soft.

If her mother were here she'd already have been angry that she'd been so clumsy as to bump into such a regal-looking gentleman, and then to have laughed so loudly.

Her smile started to fall. What must he think of her? Had she horrified him?

She didn't think so. He didn't seem horrified by her ill manners.

But then what did she know?

And besides his occasional laughter, he did seem awfully grim. He was all but glowering at her now, and a shiver raced down her spine. "I wasn't going to purchase the book," she blurted out, her tone far more defensive than she'd intended.

He blinked in incomprehension before turning his gaze back down to the novel.

When he glanced up, she could feel a fire in her cheeks. Oh drat. What must he think of her? His gaze was so bright, so piercing, and spoke of such clever intellect, she nearly wilted in the face of it.

But she'd seen him smile too. She'd heard him laugh. And that memory alone warmed her heart and soothed her nerves.

She straightened, smoothing a hand over her skirts as she reminded herself that she wasn't lying. Not precisely. She hadn't meant to purchase the novel.

Because she'd already read it.

He offered it to her, and she caught a glimmer of amusement. "Are you certain? I should not wish to take it from you if you were interested in—"

"No, no, that's quite all right," she said. "I had no interest."

Even if she'd wanted it, she would have borrowed a copy, not bought it outright.

So there. She wasn't lying.

His scrutiny bothered her all the same. His eyes were difficult to read, and the intensity there was equally wonderful and terrifying.

Did he think less of her for being interested in a gothic novel?

Her mother surely would have. Her sister would have sniffed. Her father wouldn't have noticed, for he rarely took notice of anything she did.

Rodrick would have bought it for her. That was why her brother was her favorite.

Her great aunt had allowed her to read whatever she wished, but her mother was not so lenient. She didn't like Charlotte reading novels at all—she claimed it did nothing to damper her already overactive imagination. She wasn't certain if this man, or even London society in general, shared her mother's disapproval, but there was something so very proper about this gentleman that she didn't wish to offend him.

"I shall just..." She trailed off as she started to back away again, nodding at the stack of books where she'd last seen Mary's bonnet poking out overhead.

"You really ought to read it," he said suddenly.

She stopped. She blinked. "Pardon?"

His lips curved up at the corners, and once again she was frozen. Goodness but he was handsome. And those eyes were fierce, yes, but when he smiled it took everything in her not to grin like a fool.

He held up the book. "It's really quite good."

She stared for a moment. "You've read it?"

He dipped his head. Of course, he'd read it. Didn't he just say it was quite good?

"I enjoyed it too," she said. Her cheeks heated again, but his smile made her forget all about her embarrassment.

"You've read it?" He was gazing at her like she'd written the book herself. "I'd love to hear your thoughts."

Now she was the one gazing. Surely he didn't mean it. No one ever wanted to hear her thoughts. On anything.

"I'm nearly done, Lottie," her friend called from the other side of the stacks, her tone distracted.

"What did you like best?" the gentleman asked, his voice quiet.

She swallowed hard. She'd always been the talkative sort, but right now it was hard to form a sentence.

He wanted her opinions. On a book.

It wasn't that she couldn't think of anything to say, it was that she had too much to say. About Frankenstein, yes, but also about...oh, everything.

"I'm afraid if I start talking I won't be able to stop," she admitted.

He would laugh at her. He *should* laugh at her.

He didn't laugh at her.

His smile turned even kinder, even more understanding. "I believe I would enjoy that," he said.

The door opened behind him and two older women came in. Their stares brought Charlotte back to the moment and she backed away again.

She hadn't even been introduced to this man. Her mother would have been horrified.

Not to mention her intended. Lord Thomas likely wouldn't approve of her talking to random strangers with stern features but kind, sympathetic smiles.

"I really ought to go," she whispered.

"Wait." His voice was still quiet, but urgent. "I still need to make up for my clumsiness earlier." He gestured toward her hem and she saw a tear at the hem that would easily be mended.

"It's no trouble," she said.

"Do you enjoy sweets?" he asked when she went to turn away.

She looked back in surprise. Was it her imagination or was that desperation in his voice? Heaven knew, her throat was nearly choked with despair at having to say farewell to this man who looked at her and...and *saw* her. She didn't know how else to explain it.

He arched his brows as the newcomers walked past them with curious glances.

"Sweets?" she echoed. "Who doesn't like sweets?"

This was met with a chuckle. "There's a tea shop near here," he said. "Three doors down. They have the most marvelous confections. I go there often."

"Oh, I—" She swallowed hard. Was he inviting her along?

Would she dare?

She glanced back at the stacks where her new friend was blissfully unaware of her improper behavior. Their maid who was meant to be chaperoning them had disappeared as well.

The fact that she was still standing here alone, conversing with a stranger was bad enough, no doubt. If it were just her here, perhaps. But she couldn't risk harming Mary's reputation as well.

No, she didn't dare. Especially not if it meant dragging her new friend into trouble.

"I go there most days," he said.

"It must be very good then," she said with a smile.

"Exceptional," he said. But the way he was looking at her. The way his gaze focused on her as he said it with a heat that singed her to her bones.

"I must go," she said quickly, turning so quickly she nearly tripped and fell. Again.

And wouldn't that have made for a dramatic exit to what was undoubtedly the most romantic moment of her life.

She sighed as she reached Mary, who was poring over a small stack of books before her, their poor maid who'd acted as their chaperone looking bored beyond belief as she perched on a stool in the corner.

She likely wouldn't have looked so bored if she'd realized one of her charges had toppled into the arms of a stranger.

"Everything all right?" Mary murmured, not looking up.

"Yes, of course," Charlotte said. But she was out of breath as though she'd just run, and her lungs felt tight with the urge to cry.

Silly, maudlin girl. She would not cry over parting with a gentleman she didn't even know. Even if it did seem extremely unfair that she wasn't allowed to pursue a conversation with the one gentleman who'd ever truly struck her fancy.

She fanned herself as she waited for Mary to make her decision and from where she stood she heard Lord Paul leave, along with the other ladies.

When at last Mary was ready to leave, her new friend was far too observant. "Are you sure you're all right?" she asked. "You seem distracted."

She smiled wanly. "I met a man, that's all."

Mary stopped walking and their maid nearly walked into her. "Pardon?"

"Lord Paul," she said with a smile that was admittedly dreamy. "He was lovely. Kind and thoughtful and he's even read—"

"Lord Paul?" Mary's face grew pinched. "Surely not... I would have noticed... She frowned. "Well, I *was* rather preoccupied..."

Charlotte waited patiently for Mary to cease speaking to herself. "You know of him?"

Mary tilted her head to the side as if seeing Charlotte for

the first time. "Surely not Lord Paul, the son of the Earl of Galena?"

She remembered the shopkeeper's words about sending his regards to Lady Galena.

"That's the one," she said with a grin. She'd never been good at staying despondent for long.

Besides, if fate were real and some sort of romantic destiny was in her future, she'd see him again. Of that she was certain.

The fact that Mary seemed to know of him was proof enough that she would see him again.

Charlotte glanced over at her friend and blinked in surprise.

The fact that Mary was puckering her lips as if she'd tasted something awful wasn't quite as good of an omen.

"Why are you making that face?" Charlotte asked.

"Lord Paul is not lovely. Nor is he kind or thoughtful or—"

"So you know him?" Charlotte perked up. Perhaps she would get her introduction after all.

"You could say that." Mary's answer was cryptic, yes, but Charlotte was determined.

"Tell me everything," she said.

It seemed Lord Paul had grown up in the countryside near Mary's family estate and the rest of the way home Mary regaled her with stories of childish pranks and silly jests that had Charlotte laughing even as Mary sulked.

"So bad behavior as a child then," Charlotte said when they reached the school. "I do believe the same could have been said about me."

Mary lifted a shoulder in a pragmatic gesture. "I suppose you're right. But please do remember that you already have a suitor, and Lord Paul..." She wrinkled her nose. "Well, from what I've heard, Lord Paul is quite the flirt."

"Truly?" Charlotte couldn't imagine it. Had he flirted with her? Maybe a little. But it was not the gregarious, smiley sort of charm she'd expect from a rake or a libertine. It was mild teasing, hidden smiles.

He was understated and a mystery, which made her like him that much more.

She always had loved a good mystery.

"Well, I suppose there was no harm done," Mary continued. "It's not as though you're likely to run into him again, now is it? We hardly move in the same circles."

Charlotte's insides fell with disappointment.

She supposed Mary was right. But she was still despondent when Miss Farthington called out to her from the drawing room when they walked through the front door. "Ah, just who I was hoping to see."

"They were sorry to have missed you," Miss Farthington said, handing her a calling card. "Lord Thomas, in particular."

Her gaze held a question that Charlotte ignored. She was certain her mother had told the headmistress about her situation when she'd enrolled her here. Most likely she'd asked that their every class in music, decorum, and the like all be with Lord Thomas in mind.

She thanked Miss Farthington with a weak smile before heading back to the staircase. The calling card seemed to weigh heavily in her hand.

It was just a matter of time before he'd call again.

Which meant it was just a matter of time before he went from an intended suitor to her very real fiancé. And then she'd be trapped. Forever.

"Everything all right, Lottie?" Mary asked when she rejoined her at the stairs leading to their rooms.

"Of course." But her smile and good cheer couldn't keep at bay this feeling that a noose was tightening around her neck.

But she'd bought herself time, hadn't she?

She stared down at the card as her mind raced.

She might as well make the most of it.

"I wonder what's going on in that head of yours," Mary teased. "Not planning some mischief are you?"

Charlotte choked on a laugh. Goodness but it was nice to have a friend. "Perhaps," she said coyly.

"Do tell," Mary said as they linked arms heading up the stairs.

"I was just thinking that I'd like to take an outing soon. I find I'm ravenous for some sweets."

Mary shot her a quizzical glance, but she didn't ask questions.

Which was for the best. Her new friend wasn't in the same predicament so she likely couldn't understand.

After all, fate and destiny were all fine and good. But when a young lady had a noose hanging over head and time was running out...

Well, sometimes destiny just needed a helping hand.

CHAPTER FOUR

Thomas took a sip of his tea. The confectionaries had been delightful. Just as they'd been delicious the last two days when he'd come here for his afternoon tea.

The young girl behind the counter was eying him oddly but looked away with a blush when he met her stare.

Had Paul been right? Was he truly intimidating?

He didn't want to think so, but these past few days he'd done little but stew over it. Was he like his father?

And was that why the charming young Lottie hadn't made a trip to this tea shop?

Or perhaps she had and he'd missed her.

He set his cup down with a rattle. Curse it. Why hadn't he asked for her full name? Or her address so he might call upon her?

Aside from the fact that it would have been wildly improper, of course. But then, everything about their encounter had been wildly improper. What was one more gaffe?

But then there was the fact that he already had a young lady whom he was supposed to be courting.

He sank low in his seat as he pulled out the missive he'd received from Miss Charlotte the other day shortly after his run-in with his enchanting and bookish girl of his dreams.

He cringed as he read her tidy script again. As if this time perhaps her words wouldn't be quite so repugnant.

Dear Lord Thomas,

My deepest apologies for being unable to attend to you and your mother. I fear I was ordered to bed upon suffering from a fit of the vapors, the likes of which have never been seen. 'Tis the air, I believe. Far too much sunshine here in London for my delicate nerves.

It went on, and on, and then on some more. All to say that she was unwell and not up for visitors anytime soon.

Which was a relief. Or would have been if this note had not confirmed his worst fears about the woman who was to be his wife.

He pinched the bridge of his nose as he recalled her mother's last visit in excruciating detail. Was she somehow worse off than her mother? Was her constitution so delicate that she was an invalid?

Perhaps he ought to pity her if that were the case.

Yes. He should surely pity her. It wasn't her fault she was ill. But then...

His brows drew together as he read her note again. How could anyone claim that London had too much sunshine?

He glanced out the window at the dreary afternoon sky. Then he tucked the missive back in his pocket. Staring at it was just one more reminder that his being here was folly. Only the worst sort of fool would behave as he had done.

Coming here every day in the hopes that she might arrive? It was lunacy.

He scrubbed a hand over his jaw and dropped his head into his hand.

"Why, what a surprise." A familiar female voice at his side had his head coming up abruptly.

His heart nearly flew out of his chest at the sight of her.

Her.

Lottie.

Finally.

Her smile was sweet but hesitant. "Perhaps you do not recall but I was the lady you bumped into the other—"

"Of course!" He stood abruptly, his chair scraping against the wooden floor in his eagerness to stand and bow to her and the maid who hovered behind her. "How lovely to see you again."

Her smile bloomed and he felt it like a jolt to his heart. Looking around at the small shop pointedly, she said, "I have it on good authority that they have wonderful confections here."

His heart up and melted in his chest. She'd come here in the hopes of seeing him. At least, he assumed that was what she meant, and just like that he no longer felt like such a fool.

"Please," he said. "Have a seat."

The shop was crowded and seats were in limited supply. Surely it would be all right to visit with her maid so close by. Just for a moment.

Even as he tried to justify his actions, Lottie was taking her seat with a grateful smile and he realized...he did not care.

The justifications and rationalizing were happening by

rote in his mind, but truly, he could not bring himself to care about his father's lectures or society's disapproval.

For once he wanted to thumb his nose at all the rules. His days were numbered, after all. This dalliance might not be able to last, but it was his one taste of freedom and romance, and he meant to make the most of it.

"Allow me," he said before fighting his way through the crowd to the counter where he ordered her a selection of everything they had available.

When he returned, she was smiling warmly, and who needed sunshine when this lady was near? Everything about her spoke of warmth and joy, from the sweet curve of her pink lips, to the dimples that formed when it grew into a wide smile as he sank into the seat across from her.

So very beautiful. But not in that untouchable way of the young ladies he'd been forced to dance with when he was dragged along to a ball. She had the sort of beauty that eased a tension in him he hadn't realized was there. Looking upon her was like drawing in a deep breath of fresh air. Her blonde locks piled high on her crown were the golden hue of an afternoon sun and her creamy complexion and pink cheeks seemed to speak of long walks and dancing freely in the open air.

At what point his thoughts had become quite so poetic and nonsensical, he had no idea. It seemed to be a direct result of her proximity.

"This is all very scandalous, isn't it?" she asked, but her voice wasn't afraid, it was excited.

"It is, I suppose." He couldn't stop a grin of his own.

"You have a wonderful smile," she said.

"Funny, I was just thinking the same of you."

She blushed. "No, truly. It's a wonder. Without it you are one man, but when you smile you transform into someone else entirely."

He arched a brow. No one had ever said as much before. "Tell me," he said as he leaned forward to be heard. "What did you think of *Frankenstein?*"

Of all the things he wished to discuss with her, this seemed the most harmless. It was a book. Fiction. There was nothing wrong with discussing literature, was there?

But when she burst out talking, words tumbling out of her mouth and off her tongue so quickly he had to concentrate to keep up—it was then that he realized he'd been wrong. For a man who loved books, hearing her talk about literature was everything.

Listening to this lovely, vivacious lady speak so eloquently about books was like falling in love.

His pulse raced as he nodded and murmured his agreements. When she paused long enough to ask for input, he wasted not a second to fill the air with his thoughts and his theories.

Truly, he'd never spoken more in his life than he did during those brief moments when she paused expectantly, as if she were eagerly awaiting his response.

It was beautiful.

It was magic.

"Isn't it strange that we both came to the same conclusion?" she said breathlessly. "And we've never even met before today."

It was lunacy.

He straightened with a start as her words jarred him out of his reverie. He'd lost himself so thoroughly he'd nearly forgotten how improper this was.

He glanced around them as if his parents or hers might come leaping in to separate them. Well, maybe not *her* parents. He had no notion what her family was like. Her maid didn't seem to notice much of anything as she worked away on her knitting at the neighboring table.

But his father... If he had the slightest suspicion that Thomas was meeting with strangers to discuss books while he ought to be planning his next visit to that finishing school of Miss Charlotte's—

"...and so I really must get back to the School of Charm," Lottie was saying.

Thomas blinked. He'd missed something. "Pardon?"

A blush crept into her cheeks. "I was just saying that nearly an hour has passed and I really should be returning."

A knot formed low in his gut. He could have sworn she'd mentioned the finishing school that Miss Charlotte attended. "Get back where, exactly?"

Oh blast, that came out wrong.

Her cheeks stained pink and he realized she probably thought he was asking for her address.

"I just meant—"

"The School of Charm?" she said at the same time. It came out as a question, and she gave him a shy, hesitant smile. A rare hint of vulnerability from this intoxicating, brazen, whirlwind of a lady. "It's a finishing school nearby. That's where I live at the moment."

His stomach sank to the floor. Surely not. That was where Miss Charlotte lived.

Charlotte.

Lottie.

He stared at her with parted lips as blood rushed past his ears, drowning out the sounds of the tea shop.

Surely not.

Hope flared hot and terrifying. *Are you Miss Charlotte Haverford, daughter of Lord Meagher?*

He couldn't get the words out. Because if he was wrong...

But then again, if he was right...

"To think, Lord Paul," she said sweetly, her smile small and intimate, like they were the oldest of friends. "We've been talking as if we've been friends our whole lives, yet..." She glanced about her furtively before whispering. "We haven't even been properly introduced."

"Lord Paul," he repeated woodenly, his gut churning with unease.

Blast. He'd forgotten entirely that she'd mistaken him for Paul the other day. He should have corrected her right then and there, but he hadn't and now she thought—

"Yes, I recall your name," she said with a laugh as she stuck out a hand as if to shake his.

He blinked. Had he just accidentally done it again? He'd repeated the name out of shock and yet to her it must have seemed as though...

Oh dear.

She thought he was finally introducing himself.

He took her gloved hand in his. How could he not? He held it gently, stroking the back of her fingers as he tried to think of how he might explain this confusion about his name, while also asking her for *her* name in return.

He flinched inwardly. He truly had gone about this all wrong.

Maybe this was why his parents were so keen on him being so dashedly proper. To avoid awkward situations like this one.

He nearly laughed aloud at the thought. As if anyone could have predicted *this* predicament. He cleared his throat, "Miss, please—"

"Oh, it's Miss Charlotte," she interrupted with a wide grin.

His hopes burst into flight even as his belly twisted in horror at having to explain that he was the man she was supposed to marry.

He stared at her in shock all over again. She was the woman he was to marry.

His heart collided with his ribcage as that thought registered throughout him, spreading through his limbs and into his veins like liquid gold, hot and brilliant.

It couldn't be true.

It couldn't be her. It just *couldn't.*

He'd never been so lucky in his life, and besides... His free hand moved to the pocket where he'd stashed Miss Charlotte's letter, unable to reconcile the tedious lady who had penned that missive with the darling sweetheart before him.

"You...you live at the finishing school, you say," he managed.

Maybe there were two Charlottes there.

"That's right, I just arrived back in London, you see. I'd been traveling with my great aunt."

Perhaps there were two Charlottes who'd just recently arrived back in England?

He swallowed hard, his pulse pounding as his mind zigged and zagged trying to sort through his racing thoughts.

This was a good thing, of course. No, that was an understatement. This was a blessed miracle. A turn of events the likes of which he never could have hoped for, let alone foreseen.

He liked his bride-to-be.

He more than liked her, if he were being honest. He was smitten. Attracted to her, yes—who wouldn't find her stunningly pretty? But it was her character, demeanor, intellect, and wit that made her the most enchanting woman he'd ever met.

"And you, Lord Paul?" she asked.

He stared at her blankly, mainly because he'd lost track of the conversation, but also because...

Blast.

She thought he was his best friend.

"Do you reside nearby?" she prodded, seemingly unaware

that with each new word she uttered, his life turned more and more on its head.

"I do, yes," he said.

She tugged her hand back and dipped her head with an adorable blush. Her spectacles hovered on a chain around her neck. He felt as though he knew this woman—as she'd said, he felt as though they'd known one another forever.

But if she truly were the young lady his parents had been telling him about, if she were Lady Meagher's daughter, if she were the one who'd written that note...

"Do you suffer headaches, Miss Charlotte?" he asked suddenly.

She blinked up at him. "Pardon?"

He cleared his throat as he pointed to her spectacles. "My mother had issues with her eyesight and she found it led to headaches."

"Oh dear, how horrible," she murmured. "But no, I have no such ailments."

"Well, that is good to hear," he said.

She smiled and gave him a regretful smile. "I really ought to get back."

He leaned forward and captured her hand again, this time making her blink in surprise. "Sorry," he said quickly, letting go of her fingers. "I just..." He cleared his throat. "I should very much like to see you again."

Her expression shifted, her smile now seeming oddly sad. His own lips curved down in a glower. He did not like to see this young lady sad.

He did not like it one bit.

"I wish that I could," she said slowly. "But I...I am afraid I cannot."

His insides crashed and they landed hard. "You cannot?"

She didn't explain, just tipped her head down, biting her lip.

It clicked at once. She thought he was Paul. She didn't know that she was talking to the man she was meant to wed. "Miss Charlotte, before you leave, you must know—"

"No, please," she said quickly. "We've already said too much. I already feel too much, truth be told."

"You do?" He could hardly breathe he was so happy.

Oh joyous day, she felt it too.

"But this is wrong," she said, her voice grim. "I should not have let us go on like this. You see—"

"Miss Charlotte, please—"

"I have an understanding with another gentleman," she said quickly, her gaze darting about as if she were indeed guilty of some crime.

"You do," he said slowly, his mind trying and failing to figure out how best to break this news to her.

Before he could, she leaned forward over the table with wide eyes and a tragic sigh. "But I do not want to marry him."

He blinked. "You don't?"

"He's awful, I'm sure of it," she hurried on.

His head jerked back as if he'd been slapped. "He is?"

"He must be," she said.

"Have you..." He cleared his throat. Well. This was not a fortuitous start to this conversation. When he finally spoke, he chose his words carefully. "Do you know your suitor well then?"

She pouted. "No. But I know what he's like."

He felt the urge to laugh rising up. "Oh, my dear Miss Charlotte—"

"He's intimidating and boring and overbearing and—" She sniffed. Tears welled in her eyes. "And I truly do not wish to marry him."

The air was sucked from his lungs. Intimidating? Was he really that bad? And boring, well...he supposed he might be that.

"Perhaps," he started and stopped. "Er, perhaps..."

He let his words trail off. She stared at him with such despair, he couldn't bring himself to inform her that he was...well, *him*.

"Perhaps you ought to give him a chance," he said.

She blinked, swallowing hard.

He felt a blow to his chest at the stricken look in her eyes. She looked at him as though he'd disappointed her.

"Miss Charlotte—"

"You're right, of course," she said quickly, coming to her feet before he could stop her.

"I didn't mean—"

"You speak sense, that's all. I'm grateful for it." But she wouldn't meet his gaze, not even when he escorted her and her maid to the door.

"Miss Charlotte," he started again.

"I do hope I see you around the neighborhood some time, my lord." She gave a quick curtsy before running away. Or at least walking so swiftly that her poor maid struggled to keep up.

He ran a hand over his hair with a groan. Well, that had gone badly.

Very, very badly.

He'd managed to muck it up as Lord Thomas *and* as Lord Paul.

He kept watching her until she turned a corner. Back to the finishing school. Where she'd be waiting for Lord Thomas to come visit her.

He grimaced as he turned back toward his own home.

How exactly was he going to get himself out of this mess?

CHAPTER FIVE

Mary rested her head on Charlotte's shoulder as they walked out of the classroom. "That was exhausting," she moaned.

"Was it?" Charlotte teased. "I thought it was a lovely lesson."

Mary lifted her head to scowl at her. "That's because you are already fluent in French. You and Monsieur Dupres must have had a fine conversation, but all I understood was that you both agreed that the weather was miserable."

Charlotte laughed and patted her arm. "We'll practice together later, shall we? After you've had some time to rest that quick mind of yours."

"It didn't feel so quick today," Mary muttered.

Charlotte smiled. Her friend was being humble. Nearly a fortnight of being the only two students at the School of Charm as Miss Farthington awaited her new arrivals, and Charlotte had come to learn that Mary wasn't just intelligent. She was remarkably sharp. When it came to mathematics and philosophy—even music—Mary was extremely knowledgeable and what she did not know already she picked up quickly.

It was only languages that taxed her clever mind, and that happened to be the one area where Charlotte excelled.

Well, that and literature. But it had become clear quickly that the sort of novels she enjoyed were not what any of their tutors and governesses wished for her to talk about during lessons in elocution and decorum.

Miss Farthington didn't mind, though. She was far from the stern headmistress Charlotte had feared she'd be. Perhaps it was because she was still quite young, and had a bit of scandal to her name, but Charlotte found the woman to be quite sympathetic toward her younger charges.

Their headmistress was heading in their direction as they made for the stairs. "How was your lesson, ladies?" she asked with a bright smile.

"Wonderful," Charlotte answered.

Mary kept silent. She wasn't much of a liar.

"Mary, a letter arrived from your sister," Miss Farthington said. "And Charlotte, you've been quite popular this morning. Messengers arrived with a missive and a package for you."

Charlotte's smile fell. There was only one person in this town who'd been sending her a note by messenger. Though a gift from her intended would be a first.

She and Lord Thomas had been corresponding through letters ever since she'd responded to his visit with a note of apology for not being able to receive him. Her parents and his were showing a certain amount of leniency in this regard, allowing them to communicate directly—just another sign that in their minds this engagement was as good as official.

Charlotte could admit his messages were cordial, if stiff. His missives only confirmed that he was as proper and dull as she'd been led to believe. He was polite in his regards concerning her health. Though he somehow managed to sound pompous with those few terse lines about how he hoped she'd be feeling well enough to receive him next time he called.

But he hadn't called again, thank heavens. Instead, he'd sent a note crying off for his planned visit, claiming urgent business that required his attention and so began another round of formal, dull notes being exchanged.

Charlotte tried to make up for his dullness by making hers as ridiculous as she could manage without being obvious. It wasn't much of a consolation for being trapped in a match she did not wish, but amusing herself did cheer her spirits.

"What could he have sent?" Mary asked as they followed Miss Farthington to her study. Mary's tone was filled with excitement.

Neither of them received many letters or packages from their families, as the whole reason they were there was to be out of the way, which was just another way of saying forgotten. She couldn't blame Mary for being excited, but she also wasn't keen to receive anything from her soon-to-be fiancé.

Gifts meant she'd feel compelled to be at home for visitors next time he and his mother called. She sighed warily as she trailed into the small, cozy room behind the headmistress and Mary. She supposed she couldn't put it off much longer anyway.

And what for? It wasn't as though there were some other gentleman pining for her. Her lower lip trembled as the image of a tall, sandy-haired, stern-featured gentleman filled her mind's eye.

Perhaps you ought to give him a chance.

She scowled at the fire in the fireplace as Mary opened her letter and began to read. She knew quite well she was being unreasonable, and Mary had told her so time and again.

Much as I dislike agreeing with anything Lord Paul might have to say, she'd said with a crinkle of her nose after Charlotte had wept on her shoulder. *You must see that he has a point.*

And yes, logically she did understand that what they'd been doing was wrong. Scandalous, even. Guilt niggled at her whenever she thought of just how much trouble they might have caused if anyone had learned of their rendezvous.

But even so, his words had felt like a betrayal.

She'd been so sure Lord Paul had felt the same way. But if he were pushing her into the arms of another man—even if it was the man she was meant to marry—then clearly he had not shared her feelings.

Miss Farthington offered Charlotte the letter first, and Charlotte accepted it grudgingly, unsealing Lord Thomas's note with all the eagerness of one headed for the gallows.

Of course, Lord Paul had a point. Just because they could talk at length about books didn't mean he was going to disrupt her parents' plans for her marriage. And for all she knew, he had an arrangement of his own.

Her hands stilled as she broke the seal, her stomach dipping in horror at the thought of Lord Paul marrying another.

Was that why he had urged her toward Lord Thomas?

Perhaps. She had no way of knowing what his situation might be. Mary was no help there. All she knew of Lord Paul was from their childhood together. And neither she nor Charlotte had been out in society long enough to be privy to the latest gossip either, so Charlotte was left to speculate and imagine what Lord Paul had been thinking.

Had he truly not felt it? This connection she'd thought was as strong and sure as the ground beneath her feet. She'd been so sure when his eyes met hers, when his firm, harsh mouth eased into a smile that felt meant for her and her alone—she'd been so sure that he'd been feeling it too.

With a sigh she finally opened the letter and scanned it quickly.

She and Lord Thomas had gone back and forth with their messages enough times for her to recognize his decisive handwriting. She pursed her lips in distaste.

Even his handwriting was imposing and awful.

"What does Lord Thomas say?" Mary asked. Apparently, she'd finished reading her own correspondence.

Charlotte forced a smile. "He will not be attending the masquerade after all."

Mary's face fell. "Oh, that is a disappointment."

Miss Farthington too was wincing slightly as if Charlotte must be disappointed by this news. The masquerade marked their families' latest attempt to thrust them together, and Charlotte felt nothing but relief that she was spared once more from the dreaded meeting that would mark the end of her freedom.

Neither of her two new friends seemed to fully understand just how much she was dreading her first meeting with her intended. They believed that she must be curious, at the very least. Both had said so multiple times.

But Charlotte wasn't curious. Not about him. Truly, she had barely a thought to spare for Lord Thomas as she was too preoccupied wondering what Lord Paul was thinking.

Had he forgotten about her already?

Probably.

She was no doubt one of many ladies who'd fallen for his charms. Hadn't Mary said he was known to be a flirt?

She wearily reached for the small package that had arrived for her today as well. She was starting to believe Mary had been right all along. Lord Paul was indeed a terrible rake. Made even more dangerous precisely because his style of charm was so subversive.

It had seemed like it had been just for her. Like perhaps with everyone else he brooded and scowled, but the mere sight of her brought out his smile.

Silly nonsense. She gave her head a shake, only dimly aware of Mary and Miss Farthington's laughter and chatter as she once again lost herself in thoughts of Lord Paul.

Charlotte was a bit too harsh tearing off the string that bound the wrapped present.

She was beginning to wish she'd never met that beastly Lord Paul. He'd tricked her into thinking he had feelings for her. He'd made her believe she was special in his eyes. She tore off the string and clawed at the wrapping. He'd made her swoon over him, and then he'd had the nerve to—

Send her a book.

She blinked, her lips parting on a gasp that was so loud, Mary and Miss Farthington fell silent.

She opened the copy of *Frankenstein; or the Modern Prometheus* to find a flower pressed between the pages and she choked on a sob and a laugh before she could stop it. A small scrap of parchment fluttered to the ground, and in a scrawl quite similar to Lord Thomas's was a simple message.

I am sorry for the way we parted. I dearly wish to see you. I shall be at the masquerade. If you are in attendance, I shall find you. Yours.

No signature. No name.

But she did not need one. She knew very well who'd sent it and every cruel thought she'd harbored against Lord Paul was forgotten as she pressed the book to her chest.

"What did Lord Thomas send you?" Mary asked.

"Oh!" She lifted her head quickly, a flush of guilt creeping up her neck as the other two ladies waited expectantly.

"It was a present from a friend, actually," she said, quickly tucking the copy of *Frankenstein* behind her back.

Fortunately, they were interrupted by a servant announcing visitors for Charlotte.

This time she didn't even think of hiding because she knew without a doubt it was not Lord Thomas. And indeed, even as she headed past the servant toward the drawing room she heard the maid tell Miss Farthington, "Lady Meagher, miss, and her son, Lord Henley."

Charlotte picked up her pace. Rodrick was here! "Come, Mary," she called back. "You must meet my brother."

And her mother, of course. That went without saying.

Her mother greeted her with a tight smile as Rodrick held out his arms for an embrace. "Good to see you, Lottie."

She pressed her face into his chest with a grin. He'd become quite the dashing young viscount while she was away, and it was still a shock to see him so grown and mature.

Charlotte introduced them both to Mary as Miss Farthington poured tea for the visitors. Lady Meagher had never been particularly maternal. She loved her children, of that Charlotte was certain, but she was not given to displays of warmth and affection, and so it was not a surprise to her that her beautiful, blonde, still youthful looking mother did not ask after her studies or her happiness.

"Still no introduction to Lord Thomas," she said instead. It wasn't a question. Her mother and Lord Thomas's were acquaintances, and Lady Meagher had been quick to learn about Charlotte's illness which had left her indisposed to visitors.

Her mother had sent a withering message about how her health had best improve quickly. The 'or else' was implied.

Charlotte's mother made her blush as she not so subtly inquired about Mary's connections and her family.

"Mother, please," she murmured.

But Mary being Mary seemed unfazed and answered every question in that forthright way she had that Charlotte so adored. It truly was a wonder to find a lady so disinclined to artifice and subterfuge. She'd feared the young ladies she met at the School of Charm would be manipulative or terribly tepid in character, but Mary was the exact opposite of what she'd expected.

She saw that Rodrick, at least, enjoyed her candor as well. She was almost sorry that her brother was so happily matched with Miss Fanny Harper. While she'd heard nothing but praise for Miss Harper, she'd relish the chance to have Mary as an actual sister.

But alas, while he and Miss Harper's father had not yet formalized their arrangement, it was understood that by the end of this season he would propose to her.

"How is Miss Harper?" she asked when her mother and Mary were caught up in a conversation about her father's lineage that was threatening to bore Charlotte to tears.

The smile that tugged at her brother's lips was so endearing, Charlotte barely swallowed a giggle in time. "She's perfect, as always," he said. "I find I am impatient to make our arrangement official, but I do not wish to rush her."

Rodrick shared her fair hair and blue eyes, and had the same tall, slender build as their father. But he'd filled out while she'd been on the continent, his shoulders broader, his chest more robust. He was well and truly grown, and clearly keen to start a family of his own.

She wasn't even sure he knew just how dazed and besotted he looked at the mere mention of Miss Harper's name. "Does your Miss Harper know that you're in love with her?" she asked.

He sputtered on his tea before swallowing and shooting

her a narrowed-eyed glare. "Charlotte, what sort of question is that?"

She arched her brows. "An honest one."

She glanced over to catch a wink from Mary, who'd apparently overheard.

Rodrick cleared his throat, his gaze darting about, not meeting hers. "No, she does not know. And she likely never will."

"Why not?" she demanded.

He sighed in exasperation. It was a sound she was well used to from her family members, even her beloved Rodrick. "Because, Charlotte, while Fanny and I have formed a wonderful friendship, I don't think...that is, I do not believe..." He glanced around them again as if seeking help, but their mother and Miss Farthington were now discussing the season's fashion trends as Mary pretended to listen while reaching for a biscuit from the serving tray a maid had just now brought in.

"Well?" Charlotte prompted. Her brother had always been her closest ally, the only relative aside from Aunt Ida who actually seemed to like her and not just tolerate her because she was a member of the family. She wanted to see him happy. He of all people deserved to be happy.

He sighed, giving her a baleful look. "She doesn't feel the same, that's all." He flashed her a small, stoic smile. "Not yet, at least."

Charlotte wished to argue. Who wouldn't love her loveable, handsome, kindhearted brother? But as she'd never met this woman, she couldn't exactly speak on her behalf. "When will I get to meet her?" she asked instead.

"Meet who?" her mother interrupted.

Rodrick answered for her. "Charlotte is eager to meet Miss Harper."

Her mother huffed as she murmured, "If only she were so eager to meet her own betrothed."

"He's not my betrothed yet," she said quickly.

She did not miss the glare that her mother shot in Miss Farthington's direction, nor the way her headmistress avoided that look by sipping her tea and feigning not to notice.

This was why Miss Farthington was such a dear. Charlotte had no doubt her mother was pressuring Miss Farthington to assist her in her attempts to get Charlotte in the same room with Lord Thomas.

Although, in Charlotte's defense, Lord Thomas had been making it frightfully easy to avoid him. He seemed just as keen to avoid their first meeting as she was.

She shifted in her seat. She wasn't certain how she ought to feel about that.

"Yes, well," Rodrick said with that peacekeeping tone he was so adept at wielding. "Perhaps Charlotte will be able to meet both Miss Harper and Lord Thomas at the upcoming masquerade."

Charlotte straightened, excitement flooding through her. She'd always wanted to attend a masquerade and for months now she'd been waiting for this chance. This public masquerade was held every year at the start of the season and her family always attended. This year she'd finally be able to join them. The idea of a masquerade had always appealed to Charlotte. It sounded so delightfully romantic.

And now that she knew Lord Thomas would not be in attendance, and more importantly, that Lord Paul *would* be there, waiting for her...

"Oh yes, please, Mother. I should so love to attend," she said.

Her mother's brows drew together in confusion. "Of course,

you'll attend. I've already promised Lord Thomas's mother that you'll be there. Your father and I won't be able to make it—that dreadful house party falls on the same day, unfortunately. But Charlotte, you must attend." Her mother glared at her. "You'll not avoid this encounter any longer, young lady."

She opened her mouth to protest. "Oh, but he will not—" She stopped abruptly. Lord Thomas had only sent that note today. It seemed her mother had not yet learned the Lord Thomas was crying off from this outing. She kept her lips pressed together firmly.

Surely it wasn't her place to explain Lord Thomas's agenda, now was it?

Her mother arched her brows. "What was that?"

"Er..." She glanced over at Mary and Miss Farthington. They met her gaze evenly. Miss Farthington continued to sip her tea and Mary gave her another knowing wink. Charlotte's heart swelled with gratitude at having found two such dear and wonderful compatriots. They knew quite well that Lord Thomas would not be in attendance.

But Lord Paul would.

She folded her hands demurely and adopted her most innocent expression. "Nothing, Mother."

Her mother gave a satisfied harrumph. "Well then, we'll finally make this engagement official. Mark my words," she added to no one in particular. "By the end of the season I expect to have all three of my children happily engaged."

Charlotte shared a look with Rodrick, who gave her a grimace of commiseration. None of Lady Meagher's children had been free to choose a spouse for themselves. And yet, she was the only one who seemed to mind.

"Will Eloise be joining us at the masquerade?" she asked.

Her mother's lips pursed as she considered this. "If Lord Pickington wishes her to."

Charlotte shuddered, but no one seemed to notice. *If he wishes.*

That would be her life soon enough too.

No freedom, and a life spent obeying to the stern dictates of an overbearing bore. She sighed as she set down her teacup and forced that thought to the side.

After all, Lord Thomas would not be at this masquerade.

Only Lord Paul.

And who knew what might happen when they met again?

She ducked her head to hide a smile.

A masquerade was the perfect place to declare their feelings. And he did share her feelings. Of that she was almost certain.

CHAPTER SIX

Paul was eyeing Thomas with narrowed eyes. "This is truly the worst idea you've ever had."

Thomas ignored him as he adjusted his mask in the mirror.

"No, it's more than that," Paul continued. "It's the worst idea either of us has ever dreamt up, and that is really saying something."

Thomas cast his friend a sidelong glare. "You agreed she needed to know the truth. I ought to have told her last week." He paused as he fidgeted with his cravat. "Honestly, I should have introduced myself the moment she fell into my arms at the booksellers, but as I failed to do so, tonight will have to do."

Paul scrubbed a hand over his face with a groan. "There are so many ways you could explain yourself," he said, ticking them off on his fingers. "You could arrive at that finishing school as Lord Thomas and let her see for herself that you are one in the same. You could send her a letter explaining the whole ridiculous misunderstanding—" He paused to add, "I'd opt for that, by the by. Far less chance of having a candlestick thrown at your head."

Thomas sighed.

"Or you could go to her parents and—"

"No," Thomas said firmly. "I am certainly not going through her parents. And I've already told you, if I show up at her school looking like me and announced as Lord Thomas, well..." He threw his hands out, dismayed at the mere thought of the hurt he knew he'd see in her eyes. "I cannot do that to her. The shock alone would be painful, and if she thought for one second that I'd deliberately duped her..."

He couldn't even finish, the thought was so unbearable.

Paul leaned back against the wall beside an end table. He hadn't yet donned his mask so there was no disguising his doubt and derision when it came to this plan. "And you think that revealing yourself to her tonight while in disguise is the better plan?"

"I do," he said staunchly. He'd had nigh on a fortnight to think through how he could tell her the truth, and this plan had seemed fitting...in an admittedly odd sort of way.

Paul's expression clearly said he mightily disagreed.

"A masquerade is the perfect place to reveal our true selves," he added.

"Is it? Because it seems rather convoluted and more than a little silly," Paul said.

"You wouldn't understand," Thomas said. "It will be romantic."

Paul arched a brow. "I had not realized romantic meant foolish. I stand corrected. This is a brilliant plan."

Thomas looked over his shoulder to glare. "The guests should have all arrived by now."

His mother had left already with her friends. His father never attended such things. Unless he was the host or it was an event being hosted by a close friend, his father eschewed anything that did not involve shooting or riding. "Shall we order my carriage, or did you wish to walk?"

"Let's walk," Paul said, already heading toward the townhouse's front door. "Perhaps during our stroll I'll manage to talk some sense into you."

Thomas sighed. Not likely. He'd been restless with impatience these last few days. He needed to see her. He had to get this over with. The more time that went on that she didn't know, the worse he felt.

Tonight was his best opportunity to tell her not only who he was but also how he felt.

Paul would never understand because Paul had never been in love. And that was precisely what this was. It had to be. There was no other explanation for the way he couldn't rid himself of thoughts of her.

Somehow during their brief encounters, she'd burrowed inside his chest and made a home for herself in his heart.

It was most inconvenient, really. But he wouldn't have it any other way. For this was surely fate at work. It was nothing short of a miracle that the woman he loved just happened to be the woman he was meant to marry.

True to his word, Paul spent the better part of their long walk through the crisp, cold night air picking apart Thomas's plan and trying to talk sense into him.

He made excellent points, but there was one area in which Paul was ignorant. He had never met Lottie. Or rather, Charlotte. He could not know that she, like he, had the heart of a romantic.

And so, despite his friend's protests, he turned to his friend with a rare grin when they arrived at the crowded public masquerade. "I shall tell her all at the stroke of midnight," he declared.

Paul groaned. "You didn't listen to a word I said, did you?"

Thomas ignored him, diving into the crush to find her.

"You're courting trouble, old chum," Paul called after him.

Thomas didn't reply. His friend was likely right. For the first time in his life he was not strictly following his father's wishes. Although, for once, his father's wishes were his own. But if his father had any idea just how this attachment had come about, or the scandalous means by which he'd been meeting with her alone...

Well, he didn't wish to think too much on what his father would do or say.

What mattered was that for the first time ever he was pursuing what he wanted, *who* he wanted, for himself, paying no heed to the rules and obligations by which he was bound.

It was freeing. And it was all thanks to her.

His Lottie. His Miss Charlotte. His bride to be.

Assuming all went according to plan tonight, of course.

He found her quickly. That much wasn't the problem. The problem was that she was, quite rightly, surrounded at all times by her brother and sister, as well as her sister's fiancé.

He'd met Lord Henley, Lord Pickington and his betrothed before, often enough that Thomas didn't dare get too close lest they see past the mask and recognize him.

Thank heavens for the mask, though, because he was able to keep watch on her all evening. She too wore a mask, as well as a dark, hooded cape. But her fair ringlets escaped from the hood of the cape and caught the candlelight like a ray of light in this otherwise crowded and shadowy ballroom.

He never lost sight of her. How could he when she was his own personal sunshine in the midst of a swirl of dull propriety and artifice?

Fortunately, the only member of Thomas's family in attendance was his mother.

Earlier today he'd endured his father's cutting remarks about how his older brother was too busy for trivialities such as masquerades. It was only his mother's reminders that he was to meet Miss Charlotte at this outing that had silenced the earl.

Which was a blessing. His father rarely had anything kind to say to him.

Truthfully, his father never had liked him all that much. It was a fact he'd come to understand well. His brother wasn't just the heir, he was all that his father wished for in a son. He was a natural sportsman and could spend hours at the club with a cigar and brandy, talking about horseflesh and properties, and all the other topics which made him all too glad he wasn't the elder son.

He'd have made a terrible heir.

He couldn't even manage to be the spare without annoying his father at every turn.

"How has he not met her yet?" his father demanded of his mother.

As if it were her fault. As if he was not a grown man fully capable of forging his own path in life. Or at the very least, arranging his own conversations with the potential bride of his choosing.

"She's here tonight," his mother said when he went to greet her and her cluster of friends. "I'll see that you two meet. Her mother is most anxious to make the arrangements.

"Of course, Mother."

Her expression grew hesitant. "Her mother also said..."

He arched his brows expectantly when she trailed off.

His mother forced a smile that only made her look sad. "I believe your Miss Charlotte is wary of marriage."

His throat tightened at the mix of emotions that flickered in his mother's gaze. Regrets. Bitterness. Sadness. But then her gaze lifted to his once more and she was back to a wan smile that revealed nothing. "Be kind to her, won't you?"

"Of course, Mother," he said again.

But she was no longer listening. She was quickly drawn back into conversation and Thomas was secure in the knowledge that as his mother had never met Charlotte, she would not recognize her in this masked crowd.

Even if she did, he planned to avoid his mother's every attempt to bring them together. At least until after he'd had a chance to tell Charlotte who he was.

"If you'll excuse me, Mother," he murmured when she was already well occupied by the woman next to her. She gave him a wan smile that did not reach her eyes in return.

Once she was no doubt a diamond of the first water—everyone said so—but she'd long ago seemed to have forgotten how to smile. She rarely spoke either, and as his father only ever spoke in stern commands and barked orders, their house had not exactly been filled with smiles and laughter.

Even as he thought it, he heard her. His Lottie. She was near a table where refreshments were being served, and the crowd had separated her and her sister from the rest of their friends and family.

"Come, Eloise," Charlotte was saying as he drew close. "Do not pretend with me. Are you really all right with this Pickington plan?"

Her sister was pretty. Nay, she was beautiful. Even with a mask partially covering her face, Charlotte's sister was a rare beauty. He remembered the first time he had met Charlotte's sister, while Charlotte was off traveling with her great aunt. His brother had mocked him for getting stuck with the younger, less attractive sister rather than her.

He'd shot back that his brother was just jealous because he'd have to spend the rest of his days with his nagging shrew of a wife. That had shut his brother up. And he couldn't even feel guilty. Morton had been granted the right to choose his own bride. It wasn't Thomas's fault that he'd chosen so poorly.

Older than Thomas by nearly a decade, they'd never been close. And now that he lived with that unpleasant woman who found fault with anything that caught her eye, Thomas did his best to avoid his brother's home at all costs.

But his *own* home he hoped would be the very opposite of his brother's and his father's. With Charlotte at his side, it could be a place filled with warmth and laughter.

He heard her giggle at whatever it was Eloise had said. And indeed, her sister smiled too, the smile indulgent and subdued.

That was what he remembered most about Eloise those few times they'd met. She'd been subdued. Beautiful but so quiet it was as though she didn't wish to call attention to herself.

Charlotte, meanwhile...

He felt a grin tugging at his lips when her head fell back with another laugh. She wasn't trying to call attention to herself either, but she could not stop herself from being the bright sun in this room full of dusty old moons if she'd tried.

He hoped she never tried.

He'd never let himself hold out hopes for the future because his future had already been planned.

But if he had, he knew now that this woman was what he would have hoped for. This woman was everything he'd never let himself wish for. Laughter. Passion. Mischief and cleverness and warmth and smiles and—

"I'll be right back," he heard Charlotte say as she walked away from Eloise.

This was his chance. He waited until Charlotte was just out of Eloise's view before taking her hand and walking by her side toward the dance floor. The crowd was so thick no one would be able to see their hands. She gasped and glanced up, and almost instantly beamed at him so brightly it hurt his eyes and speared his heart.

"At last," she said. Her smile was brilliant. "I was starting to fear you'd had a change of heart."

"Just waiting for the perfect moment," he said.

"For what?" she teased.

"A dance." He pulled her into his arms the moment they reached the dance floor, and she gasped as the orchestra's music swelled into a waltz.

"What if someone sees?"

He paused. For a moment he'd nearly forgotten how much she was risking for him. For *him*. She could not know, of course, that were they caught dancing together, both of their parents would likely cheer with delight.

He wasn't taking a risk at all, really. But she was risking her very reputation just to be close to him.

He was humbled. For a moment he was too humbled to speak but he hoped she could see his feelings in his eyes, in the way he held her.

She sighed with a sweet, tremulous smile. "I must admit, this is all so very romantic."

That was the plan. Midnight had come and gone while she'd been surrounded by her family. There was no time like the present. He cleared his throat. "There is something I need to tell you, Lottie," he said. "Something I should have said that very first day we met."

"Oh, Lord Paul, I know," she breathed. "I feel it too."

His heart gave a jolt of happiness and his entire body felt too tight and hot. Could this be real?

Could she really be his?

"Lottie, I—"

"No, wait," she said. "There's something I need to tell you

as well. It's..." She squeezed her eyes shut. "Let us dance. For now, at least. Let me just have this one dance. All right?"

He nodded, and for the next few moments, he let himself enjoy it too. The music, the feel of her skirts swirling against his legs. The effortless way they moved together.

Despite what she'd said about not wanting to talk, she did talk. And so did he. But not about true identities and marriage and obligations.

Oh no. His Charlotte was brimming over with stories about her travels. About the different dances she'd learned and the people she'd met.

"I should like to travel one day," he said. *With you.*

One day he would travel the world with this woman in his arms.

"Where do you wish to go?" she asked.

His words came haltingly at first. He wasn't used to talking about his own wishes for the future. According to his family, he wasn't supposed to have any—at least, not ones that did not align with his duties to the family. But Charlotte's eyes were wide and her smile warm as he told her of his dreams. The pyramids in Egypt. The Nile River in Africa. The places he'd only read about but would love to see with his own eyes.

"Oh that sounds fascinating," she said, her voice hushed and reverent.

They were dancing in a dream world, he was sure of it. The crowd was all around them, the dancers pushing in tight. But with their masks and the swell of the music, he was overcome with this sensation that it was just the two of them, alone and in his idea of heaven.

But it could not last forever, and as the music slowed, the end drawing near, he knew the time had come. The masks must come off and he could only hope and pray that the dream would continue. That she would truly be his.

His gaze caught on her lips. What would it feel like to press his mouth to hers? To hear her whisper his name and to feel her wrap her delicate arms around his neck?

"Do you know what I want?" she asked when the music came to an end.

"Tell me and I will give it to you."

"Would that you could," she said with a sad little smile.

"What is it?"

"I want to be free," she said, squeezing his hand. "I used to think that meant the sort of freedom I enjoyed with my aunt on our travels. I thought it meant having no curfew and being allowed to read whatever I want and—"

"And?" he prodded when she stopped.

The crush around them was jostling them closer together and he tugged her toward a doorway. If only he could find them a moment of relative privacy where he could confess.

She stopped to smile up at him. "And now I know that the freedom I want isn't about that at all. It's about being able to follow my heart."

His heart ached at the look in her eyes. "Lottie, that is what I need to tell you. Your future. *Our* future—"

"Charlotte," a voice called from behind them. "Charlotte, is that you? I thought I'd lost you," the voice was saying.

Charlotte looked stricken. "I must go."

"No. Wait. Not until I tell you—"

"I must go," she said again as she tugged away from him, her eyes wide with panic. "They're almost upon us."

And just like that his love was lost to him. Again. Swallowed up by the crowd, and then surrounded by her family.

And he had lost his chance.

Paul found him glowering on the sidelines later that night. "How did it go?"

"I don't want to talk about it."

Paul snickered. "Not such a great plan then?"

“Shove off,” he muttered.

Paul laughed harder. “But it was to be so romantic. What could ever have gone wrong?”

Thomas sighed, pushing away from the wall. “I’m leaving. Are you coming?”

“And miss the chance to hear about your grand reveal?”

“You’re an idiot.”

But they both knew that wasn’t true. He was the fool for missing his chance.

Again.

“I cannot wait to hear all about it.” Paul turned to him as they left the masquerade and were hit with a cold wind. “Tell me again about how romantic it was?”

Thomas sighed. “I’ll see her soon,” he said. “And next time I won’t let the moment pass me by.”

“Sounds like a plan, chum,” Paul agreed, still laughing at Thomas’s expense. “Not very romantic, mind you, but it’s a plan.”

CHAPTER SEVEN

Mary stared with wide eyes as Charlotte paced the length of her bedroom at her family's townhouse. It was so close to the finishing school that they truly could have walked if not for the inclement weather.

Mary had been shocked to discover that Charlotte's family had been so close this whole time. Her own parents were still at their country estate and would be, Mary said, until Parliament was called to session.

Charlotte's parents had rarely been able to stay still in any one place for long, one of several reasons it was easier for them to have their youngest child safely tucked away at school.

Their inability to stay put was one of few traits Charlotte seemed to have inherited. Even now she could not stand still, her whole body restless to leave this stuffy bedroom that was a painful reminder of a childhood in which she'd done little but get in trouble.

Usually that trouble was unintentional. The innocent mischief of an energetic child with an overactive imagination. But she could not say the same for her behavior at the masquerade. She'd acted in a truly scandalous manner, and that was why she hadn't immediately told her friend every detail.

Mary was turning out to be her very dearest friend. She'd hate to ruin this new friendship by horrifying her with her reckless behavior.

This was why she'd only now gotten around to telling her friends the detailed account of her evening at the masquerade. Well, that and the last few days had been consumed by errands with her mother to prepare for the upcoming season. Endless fittings at the modiste had her expecting a wardrobe full of new gowns. All of which would have been lovely and exciting if not for the fact that her mother was clearly preparing for her engagement to Lord Thomas.

Her mother was already planning the ball to announce their engagement, even though Charlotte and he had never even met. Which was her own fault, according to her mother.

She wasn't wrong.

But tonight she could avoid the inevitable no longer. Her parents were hosting a soiree for the members of the *ton* who were in town. Which, of course, included Lord Thomas and his family.

And Lord Paul?

Charlotte wasn't certain. She'd been too afraid to mention his name lest her mother begin to suspect.

It was foolish paranoia—a direct result of the guilt and shame she was suffering for the way she'd behaved at the masquerade. If anyone had caught her dancing with Lord Paul...

If her sister had come upon them one moment earlier...

Charlotte shuddered to think. But she'd promised Lord Paul she'd make this right, and she would.

Mary was with her now, and together they'd come up

with a plan. Tonight she would end this understanding with Lord Thomas once and for all.

Hopefully.

Maybe.

If she could only make Lord Thomas see reason. Which, after talking to her mother, she had reason to believe was possible.

Charlotte stopped pacing long enough to face her friend. "Well? What do you think?"

Mary's brows drew together in disbelief. "You *danced* with him?" she asked. Again. For the twelfth time.

Her friend was staring at her as though she'd lost her senses.

She probably had.

It had been horribly wrong of her, she knew that. But how could something so wrong feel so right? That was what kept nagging at her. It *was* right. Being with him felt so natural and wonderful and...right. That was the only way to describe it.

"You're missing the point," Charlotte said.

Mary narrowed her eyes, visibly attempting to focus on something other than Charlotte's shocking behavior the other night.

"Right, sorry," Mary muttered. She'd already dressed for tonight's party, and her dark brown locks framed her face so sweetly, it seemed at odds with her pinched look of concentration. "So you mean to confront Lord Thomas about this directly."

Charlotte nodded, wringing her hands in front of her as she resumed pacing. Her maid had only just left after helping her dress in this gown of her mother's choosing. It chafed and bit into her ribs, making breathing difficult. Not conducive to plotting at all.

And plot she must for her time was running out. Her

mother was livid that they had not been introduced at the masquerade.

But how could we have met? Charlotte had asked. *Lord Thomas was not there.*

Her mother had glared at her in disbelief. *Who told you that? Of course, he was there. His mother told me so. Are you calling Lady Calloway a liar?*

Oh yes, Charlotte had gotten an earful from her mother.

Certainly, it was crowded, but Lord Thomas and his mother ought to have sought you out.

Her mother didn't acknowledge the fact that if she'd been in attendance, they surely would have been introduced. She wanted her daughter off her hands but was too preoccupied with her other two children to see to it herself.

Not that Charlotte minded. Her mother's negligence had meant her own freedom. For one night at least.

She'd listened to her mother's tirade in silence, her mind turning and churning with each new revelation until she'd left that particular shopping expedition more confused than she could bear.

Lord Thomas had explicitly told her that he wouldn't be there at all, but apparently he *had* been at the masquerade just as planned.

"He lied to me, you see," she said to Mary now.

She'd said it several times and yet her clever friend couldn't seem to comprehend her meaning. Granted, she'd thrown quite a bit of information at Mary after their maids departed. It was only fair that she give the girl some time to catch up.

"Perhaps there was a change of plans," Mary said. "Maybe Lord Thomas thought he would not be able to attend the masquerade but then was able to after all, at the last minute."

Charlotte shook her head. "Lord Thomas said he would not be there to avoid having to meet me, don't you see?"

Mary's lips pursed as she thought this over. "And why exactly does this make you so very happy?"

Charlotte stopped pacing long enough to grin over at her friend. "I believe Lord Thomas does not wish to make this understanding official any more than I do."

"That's an awfully big leap," Mary said.

In that moment Mary sounded so much like Charlotte's Great Aunt Ida she widened her eyes to gape at her friend.

"What?" Mary said defensively. "It's true. You haven't even met this Lord Thomas fellow, how could you know what he's thinking? I could come up with ten different reasons why he sent that note."

Charlotte waved a hand. "Perhaps you're right. But there's no way to know for sure unless I ask him outright."

Mary bolted up from the bed. "So you are going to meet him at last?"

Charlotte nodded, her lips pressed together in grim determination. "There's no way around it. My parents and his will be at tonight's ball, and there will be no masks to hide behind."

Mary nodded. "You knew this moment would come eventually."

Charlotte exhaled loudly. "Indeed. But tonight I plan on seeing through my hunch."

Mary looked wary. "What will you do?"

Charlotte clasped her hands together. "I will appeal directly to Lord Thomas to let me out of this engagement."

Mary gasped. "What will your parents say?"

Charlotte winced. "If it comes from him, they might spare my life."

Mary's silence felt ominous.

"Say something. Please," Charlotte said.

Mary sighed. "I think this might be the most sensible plan you've had yet."

Charlotte started to smile with relief.

"Which is not saying much," she added.

Charlotte's smile fell.

"But I cannot find fault with being honest," Mary said. "If you are truly to marry this man, it would behoove you both to speak plainly, I'd think."

Charlotte nodded. "Yes. Precisely. And if I'm right in my suspicion—"

Mary gave her a dubious look.

"If I'm right," Charlotte continued with renewed vigor. "And Lord Thomas also does not wish to marry..." She trailed off because the idea of having this understanding called off was too tempting by far.

Mary was nibbling on her lip. "It could harm your reputation if he throws you over—"

"I don't care about that," Charlotte said.

"Lord Paul might," Mary said.

But Charlotte was already shaking her head. She knew quite well that what Mary said was true. But she also knew her heart. And crazy as it might sound to Mary, she knew Lord Paul's as well. Or at least, she hoped she knew his heart.

Eloise arrived in her bedroom doorway and Charlotte cast a beseeching look at Mary, who sighed in turn.

"You look beautiful, Lottie," Eloise said.

"Not as beautiful as you." Charlotte grinned as her sister blushed. Her sister was so very sweet and good. They might have been great friends if they'd had anything in common. But they were still sisters, and Charlotte hoped to call upon that loyalty tonight.

"Eloise, I must ask a favor of you," she said.

Eloise's expression grew wary, which made Mary snicker with amusement.

"What is it?" her sister asked.

Charlotte braced herself for rejection. Eloise was kind

and beautiful...and dutiful. So very obedient. She'd never even thought to protest against her engagement to Lord Pickington, even though he was nearly twice her age and had all the personality of a potted plant.

Charlotte clasped her hands together. "You've met Lord Thomas, have you not?"

Eloise frowned. "Of course."

Of course. Eloise hadn't been sent off to be a companion to an elderly aunt these past two years. She'd been here in England and out in society.

"I'd like to speak with him," Charlotte said. "Alone."

Eloise's eyes widened. "You haven't even been introduced yet—"

"Yes, but I am to marry him," Charlotte shot back. "Shouldn't that count for something?" She forced a smile to lighten her words.

Eloise wasn't fooled. Her eyes narrowed. "Why? What do you wish to discuss with him?"

Charlotte glanced over at Mary and then away quickly out of guilt. Mary would urge her to be honest, but Eloise would never understand. "I'd just like a moment to get to know him without a crush around us," she said. "I do not want my first meeting with my future husband to be witnessed by a crowded room full of gossips."

Eloise bit her lip.

"Please, Eloise," she said, reaching for her hands. "I'll be in the library. Have him meet me there."

"If you're caught—"

"If we're caught, we'll be forced to marry," Charlotte said in a wry tone. "And if we're not, we'll still be forced to marry. There's little difference, is there?"

Eloise hesitated, but Charlotte could practically see her sister's sympathy overriding her good sense.

"Please, Eloise," Charlotte whispered.

Eloise sighed. "Oh, all right." She winced. "But I'm not sure how he'll feel about this. He's very proper and very..." She pursed her lips. "Stern."

Charlotte winced. Precisely why she had to end this now. She'd never survive a life with Lord Thomas.

He likely wouldn't survive a life with her either. Perhaps she'd be doing them both a favor by ending this now before they made each other miserable.

"Thank you, Eloise," she said just as their mother entered.

"There you are," she said, sweeping in and taking both her daughters in with a critical eye. Mary too, for good measure.

"Charlotte, really," she scolded. "Get rid of those spectacles."

"But I cannot see—"

"No one needs you to see, dear, just look pretty. And those spectacles make you look like a bookish bluestocking."

"Which I am," Charlotte said, ignoring Eloise's pleading looks of warning. Poor girl was forever trying to keep the peace within their home.

Their mother huffed. "Yes, well, the less Lord Thomas knows about you before the engagement is announced, the better."

Mary flinched. Eloise winced.

Charlotte barely noticed. Her mother had never tried to hide her dislike. Why, at the modiste's, Charlotte had suggested a pale gold gown—she'd always liked yellow. It was so cheerful and sunny. Her mother had pointed out that no one cared what she liked. *The less you act like yourself, the more tolerable you'll be.*

Likely true when it came to Lord Thomas. But Lord Paul liked her just as she was.

Charlotte set her spectacles aside and her mother eyed her again with a weary sigh. "I suppose this will have to do."

Her mother left just as quickly as she'd entered, and

Eloise came over and squeezed her hand. "Don't listen to her. You look beautiful."

Charlotte smiled. "Thank you."

Her sister's expression grew grim. "And I shall speak to Lord Thomas. He ought to know the real you. Because she's wrong." Her eyes grew harder and more stubborn than Charlotte had ever seen. "She's wrong about quite a lot of things."

CHAPTER EIGHT

Charlotte's sister approached Thomas with a kind smile and a curtsy. "Lord Thomas, Lord Paul," Miss Haverford said to them after greeting his parents.

Paul's family was about somewhere as well but he'd declared that he wasn't leaving Thomas's side tonight because he didn't wish to miss a thing. By that, it was understood that he meant Thomas's demise when Charlotte realized that he was him.

He was so terribly glad he could provide such entertainment for his old friend.

"How do you do, Miss Haverford?" Thomas inquired politely when it became clear that Miss Haverford was not moving on to the next cluster of guests but was instead hovering at his side.

"I have a message for you, my lord," she said quietly, her cheeks going bright pink all the way up to her flaxen hair.

"Indeed?" Thomas said, his heart thudding painfully.

Charlotte knows. That was his first thought. She knew and she'd sent her sister to tell him she didn't wish to see him again, not as Lord Thomas or as Lord Paul.

Miss Haverford pinched her lips together before blurting out, "My sister wishes to meet with you."

He blinked. "She wishes to meet...with *me*?"

Miss Haverford's brows arched slightly. "You are meant to marry, are you not? Is it so odd that she might want a moment of privacy with you?"

He blinked again. There was a hint of surprising strength in her tone, as well as a tinge of defensiveness. "No," he said finally. "No, I suppose not. But are you certain..." He looked left and right, trying to figure out how best to phrase his question. "Is it me she wishes to see?"

She stared in incomprehension. "Yes, my lord."

She thought he was a lunatic, that much was clear.

Perhaps he was because he wasn't entirely certain who he was anymore or who Charlotte believed him to be. He cleared his throat. "I just meant..." Oh blast. There was no good explanation. "We haven't been properly introduced, that's all."

"Yes, well..." She sighed and then glanced around to make sure they weren't overheard. "I think my sister wishes to get to know her future husband better. One cannot fault her for that."

"No, indeed," he murmured.

He felt a flicker of hurt that Charlotte was planning a rendezvous with Lord Thomas. Which was obviously ridiculous. He shoved the nagging thought to the side.

"She's in the library when you have a chance to slip away," she continued quietly.

He nodded. "Thank you."

"What was that about?" Paul asked as she walked away.

"The time has come," Thomas said, his voice low and solemn.

"Could you possibly sound more dramatic?" Paul mused. "I don't think you could."

Thomas ignored him, his mind still caught on all that Charlotte's sister had said. Had she changed her mind about him? Er...the Paul version of him?

Paul was still talking. "Do you know, everyone believes you to be so very uptight and terrifying. I wonder what they would say if they knew you were a romantic given to fits of histrionics?"

Thomas choked on a laugh because his friend was teasing and he knew it. Up until Charlotte had come into his life, Paul had been the only person in the world to not only know him, but to like him for it.

Heaven knew his parents and brother didn't approve of his pastimes or his character. But he'd had Paul, and hopefully, if all went well, he'd have Charlotte too. Darling, unique, wonderful Charlotte.

If she still wanted him.

"She wants to see me," he said to Paul under his breath

Paul turned to stare at him. "She wants to see you or Paul?" He flinched. "That sounded even more absurd when I said it aloud."

Thomas let out a rueful huff. "I believe she meant Lord Thomas."

"What's with that scowl?" Paul asked.

"Nothing, it's just..." His jaw clenched. "What's she doing asking for a private rendezvous with Lord Thomas?"

Paul stared at him. "You can't possibly be jealous right now."

Thomas didn't answer.

"You do realize that you *are* Lord Thomas, don't you?" Paul asked, his voice edged with disbelief.

"But she thinks I'm Lord Paul," he said.

Paul's gaze was filled with derision.

Thomas huffed as he tugged at his cravat. Paul was right. It sounded even more ludicrous when he said it aloud.

They fell silent as Thomas's parents joined them.

"Try not to muck things up tonight, Son," his father muttered to him. "We need this union with Viscount Meagher's family."

Why? He wanted to ask, but he couldn't. Those were the sort of matters his father spoke with Morton about, not him.

He suspected it had to do with her dowry, but no one had deigned to fill him in on the specifics.

"I will do my best not to," he said instead.

His father scoffed. "You couldn't even manage to get an introduction at the masquerade the other night. I suppose you were off having fun with your friends when you ought to have been doing your duty." His father continued, but Thomas was not truly listening. His mind was already with Charlotte.

How would she react when she saw that it was him?

Unless...

Unless she already knew? He glanced around. He hadn't seen her since they'd been announced, but this was her home. The people here were her guests and her family. Surely one of them pointed him out to her.

"Are you listening to me, Son?" his father demanded.

"Yes, Father," he said, his voice just as clipped and low.

Oh yes, he'd learned well how to act like his father and talk like his father. But he would never *be* his father. Which was why he already knew what he would do if Charlotte was angry or disappointed.

He'd let her go.

If she did not want him as her husband, he would help her end this. He'd take the blame and do or say whatever it took to ensure that she had the freedom to choose her future.

"You all right?" Paul asked once his father left.

"Of course."

"Of course," Paul echoed in the same mild tone with a

hint of rueful amusement. "You've gotten quite good at that, you know."

Thomas arched a brow and Paul waved a hand toward his face. "You look just like him when you get all grim and determined like that."

Just like his father, he meant.

It wasn't a compliment.

"You worried she'll be angry?" Paul asked.

Thomas had gotten very good at letting his father's words roll off his back, but right now they were ringing and echoing. "I'm more concerned that she'll be disappointed."

Paul arched a brow and Thomas shrugged. "She might only have an affection for me simply because I'm not her betrothed."

Paul didn't answer, but that seemed to be answer enough.

Perhaps she'd just been seeking a brief dalliance. An adventure before settling into the business of marriage.

But no. She wasn't so fickle as all that. In truth, it wasn't her and her fidelity he doubted. It was himself.

When all was said and done, he was not the kind of man she'd been led to believe she'd be marrying. He was nothing like his brother or his father, nor hers, for that matter.

He was an oddity within their world. An outsider even standing here at a party that was in large part meant for him.

The Charlotte he'd met had seemed to like him for who he was, and that was a rare treasure indeed. But she liked him as he was when he was a flirtation at best. A romantic daydream and nothing more.

But once he was outed as her reality. The very man she'd been dreading to meet...

Well, he had no way of knowing how she'd react.

CHAPTER NINE

Charlotte was hovering in the darkened hallway outside the library when Mary found her.

"He's here," Mary hissed as she rushed toward her, the skirts of her pretty pale gown billowing around her.

"Lord Thomas?"

"No." Mary's brows drew together. "Er, maybe. I don't know what Lord Thomas looks like so I do not know. But I'd recognize Lord Paul anywhere."

Charlotte ignored the way Mary's nose crinkled in disgust. Clearly, she was still not convinced that Paul had matured from his childish pranks.

Truly, Charlotte didn't care if he had or not. She still enjoyed childish pranks of her own. But no matter what, she liked the man he'd grown to be, and that was all that mattered.

"Where was he?" she asked. "What was he wearing? Who was he talking to?"

But before Mary could even begin to reply, they heard male voices heading toward the hallway and Mary's eyes widened with alarm.

"Go," Charlotte said. She would not have Mary getting in trouble on her behalf. "I'll be fine alone with Lord Thomas."

"Are you sure?"

"He is to be my husband," she said. "I think I can manage one moment alone in his presence." Charlotte was already nudging her toward the back hallway that would bring her friend back to the party. Just as Mary disappeared around the corner, *he* appeared.

But it wasn't Lord Thomas who came for their assignation as she'd expected.

Her face split wide with a grin.

It was *him.*

Lord Paul, looking more dashing than ever with his perfectly fitted jacket that tapered at the waist and accentuated his broad shoulders. His light brown hair looked darker in the shadowy light, but his gaze...

Oh how his eyes lit with pleasure at the sight of her.

"It's you," she said, her breathless cry escaping before she could stop it.

He didn't stop until he was close enough to take her hands in his.

"It's you," she said again, emotions swelling in her chest. "I cannot believe it."

The warmth in his eyes tempered all the severity in his features. The strong cut of his jaw and the harsh line of his nose—all of it softened to something so warm and kind with the shift in his gaze.

It was as though he were two men at once. One that everyone else saw, and one built just for her.

"It's me," he said. "I thought perhaps you'd be...disappointed." He shook his head with a rueful smile.

"Disappointed?" Was he mad?

"You thought you were to meet someone else," he explained.

She widened her eyes. How had he known about that? He must have overheard Eloise talking to Lord Thomas.

She glanced past Lord Paul.

Lord Thomas who would be coming along to meet with her at any moment. Her heart gave a sharp tug of fear.

It would not do to have Lord Thomas stumble upon them here in the hallway. Squeezing his hands, she led him into the darkened room behind her. "Come," she whispered. "We don't have long."

And truly, much as she was so gratified to see Lord Paul here, and seeking her out, no less, she'd rather hoped to have her business with Lord Thomas over and done with before they next met.

She did not wish to talk to Lord Paul about a potential future when she was not certain she had a future to give. For as much as she might rebel within her family, she knew she could not ruin her brother and sister's chances for happiness and good standing by running off to Gretna Green with Lord Paul, no matter how tempting the thought might be.

Of course, he hadn't asked her to run anywhere. Not yet, at least. But she'd seen it in his eyes and had heard it in his voice at the masquerade. The future he dreamt of, the dreams they shared...

She swallowed hard, realizing with a jolt that they were well and truly alone.

And in the dark.

Well, it was dark but for the moonlight coming in through the windows, casting just enough light to see the warmth of affection in his eyes and the sweet curve of his otherwise hard slash of a mouth.

Goodness, how she loved that mouth.

"Are you certain you're not disappointed?" he asked.

There was a flicker of vulnerability in his eyes that cut

her to the quick. He couldn't actually believe she'd prefer to see Lord Thomas.

"Of course, I'm not," she said softly.

He released her hands to grip her waist and her hands fluttered between them before settling on his chest. It was a solid chest. A manly chest.

A far different person than the incorrigible boy Mary had known as a child. A laugh bubbled inside Charlotte at that thought. "I've heard all about you, you know," she said. "I know all about your childhood and your home in the country."

His lips quirked. "Do you?" His gaze roamed over her face as if drinking her in. "Yes, I suppose that makes sense."

He must have known she and Mary were friends if their families were so close. She couldn't wait to tease Mary about having gone and fallen for her childhood enemy.

He leaned in closer. "I must admit, I've heard precious little about you over the years."

"And why would you have? I've not even been in the country until recently." She smiled, the urge to laugh still alive inside her. *Everything* was alive inside her with him so close. Her blood seemed to heat, her muscles awake and alert, her belly fluttery with nerves, and every bit of skin too sensitive by far.

She'd never felt so fully alive in all her life.

She leaned in closer and his grip on her tightened as he tipped his head down closer. He was so close that his warm, masculine scent seemed to wrap around her.

She closed her eyes briefly. She'd never felt so alive...nor so safe.

How odd to trust someone you've only just met. How perfectly lovely to find a gentleman whose arms feel more like home than her own house ever had.

"What are you thinking, Lottie?" he asked softly, his breath fanning over her cheek.

Her smile felt tremulous as emotions she could not name made her chest tighten and her heart swell. Could he ever understand how rare it was to have someone in her life who looked upon her as though she were perfect? Who saw *her* and not her family nor her dowry nor her father's title.

He saw *her* in all her outlandish, reckless glory, and the way he looked at her made her feel cherished. He made her feel accepted and understood and...and loved.

"I am so glad I met you at the booksellers that day," she whispered through a tight throat. "And I'm even happier that you are the man who came to me tonight."

She leaned into his embrace, reveling in this rare gift of a moment. Some part of her was dimly aware that yes, of course she still needed to discuss the situation with Lord Thomas. But being here in Paul's arms, she'd never been more certain of her fate.

She belonged with this man, and she would do whatever it took to make certain Lord Thomas and her parents understood all she would give up to be with him.

His forehead rested against hers. His nose touched her cheek as he let out a sharp exhale. "I must admit, I'm relieved to hear you say so."

"Relieved?" She pulled back slightly to see his eyes.

His wry, crooked smile made her heart ache. "I was so worried you'd be disappointed. Or angry, even."

Disappointed. Her brows drew together in confusion. That was twice now he'd said as much, and it made so little sense. And angry? Her lips curved down. Whatever for?

The answer came to her quickly.

For stealing this moment that was meant to have been spent with Lord Thomas, of course.

She supposed he had overstepped, but she could not be angry that he'd given her this precious time together.

And disappointed?

Never.

But the word still nagged at her. Twice now he'd said it, and she had the uncomfortable feeling she was missing something. "Why would I be disappointed?" she asked.

He lifted a hand to touch her cheek, brushing back a curl as he drank her in with that fiercely heated gaze. "I know you did not want the understanding your parents forged on your behalf, but—"

"I don't want to talk about that," she said quickly. "Not now."

Not when Lord Thomas could be out in the hallway this very minute trying to find her so they might discuss that very same understanding.

His lips pressed together. "Very well."

She sighed. She wasn't being fair. Just like at the masquerade, she was telling him what he was and was not allowed to speak of like some sort of overbearing tyrant. "I'm sorry," she whispered. "What did you wish to say?"

His eyes grew so soft and tender. "Lottie, I want to marry you. I want you by my side. I know the manner in which this has come about has been strange, to say the least, but I would not change a thing. Not about any of it. Because the way you look at me, the way you truly see me..." His throat worked as he swallowed hard. "The means by which we've come to know one another might be unusual, but I would not change a thing."

Her heart was pounding furiously. *I want to marry you.*

Said so matter of factly as if he were commenting on the weather. Her head was so light and so dizzy, for a moment she worried she might faint.

"Lottie, my love," he whispered, so close she could feel the heat of his breath on her lips. "I want to marry you, but I would never force your hand. If you decide you don't want this..." He trailed off with a frustrated shake of his head as he sought the words.

But she didn't need any more words from him. What he'd said was more than enough. What he was offering was everything. The freedom to choose her own future. The love of a man who truly understood her.

"I choose you," she whispered.

His gaze bore into hers, his eyes darkening with emotion.

"I want you," she said, her hands clenching into the fabric of his jacket. "I choose—"

His mouth crushed hers in a bruising kiss before she could finish. His lips molded to hers and in one heartstopping moment, she was flooded with bliss. Liquid heat surged through her limbs as her heart thudded wildly at the shock of these new sensations. Warm, firm lips teased hers, at once gentle and commanding.

With one hand he cupped her cheek and his other arm wrapped snug around her waist. She was pressed against the hard length of him, and her body trembled at the rightness of it.

All thoughts of her betrothal to Lord Thomas and her duty to her family fled her mind in a heartbeat. Indeed, all thoughts entirely ceased as her world came down to the sweet sensations that ricocheted in her chest and swam through her veins.

His kiss spoke of love more eloquently than any words could manage. His embrace made her want to sink into him and entrust him with her future and her happiness without a second thought.

He pulled back with a jerk, and that was when she heard it too.

Their perfect little bubble of solitude was broken by the

sound of voices in the hallway. Mary's voice rose louder than the rest. "You're looking for Lord Thomas, you say? Why, I was certain I saw him about here somewhere."

Charlotte's eyes widened and Paul's did as well.

They couldn't be found like this.

"Lottie, let me talk to them," he started.

"No." She shook her head quickly. "Not like this."

Backing out of her family's longstanding agreement would be bad enough, but to have it ended by such a scandal as this?

She couldn't do that to her family, nor to Lord Paul.

"Go out that way," she said, pointing toward a door at the far end of the library. "I shall go out this way and distract them while you slip away."

"While I slip away? I cannot leave you to—"

"You can and you must," she interrupted in a hissed whisper. "I'll tell them I had a headache and needed the solace of a darkened room."

"You've thought this through," he said, a hint of a smile on his lips.

"Of course, I had, I was meant to meet—" She stopped short. It wouldn't do to mention another man at this particular moment. Not when her lips were still swollen from Paul's kiss.

His smile was so devastatingly handsome as he grinned down at her. "Lottie, I—"

"Go." She gave him a shove toward the other end of the library as the voices drew nearer. "And don't worry, Paul," she called after him in a soft voice that had him stopping short. He turned to face her.

"What did you just say?" His brow was furrowed in confusion.

"I will not marry Lord Thomas, no matter what they

promise," she continued, her heart doing a flip in her chest at the shock on Paul's face.

Had he truly not understood how serious she was about him?

Had he not believed her that she'd chosen him, and not Lord Thomas?

"Lottie," he said, his voice a low growl. "I *am*—"

"I will handle everything," she said quickly before throwing open the door and feigning confusion at finding guests in the private quarters.

"Oh, pardon me," the woman was saying. "I'd thought I'd seen Lord Thomas heading this way."

"I'm afraid it is just me here at the moment," she said, opening the door wide for the older woman and her friends to prove she had nothing to hide. She saw Paul slipping out of the door down the hall but only Mary spotted him as Charlotte was doing her best imitation of her mother. "Oh, dear me, the pain," she moaned as she pressed the back of her hand to her forehead.

Mary turned to watch Paul hurry around the corner and then turned back to her with an arched brow as if to say, *what have you done now?*

Charlotte flinched at the thought of how she'd explain. While she was supposed to have been ending one engagement, she'd gone and become engaged to another.

"Miss Mary," one of the women called. "Do see your friend to her rooms. She ought to lie down for a while."

"Yes, of course, Lady Calloway," Mary said brightly, stepping past the women to come to Charlotte's side.

Lady Calloway. Lord Thomas's mother. So that was the woman who was supposed to be her mother-in-law.

She wouldn't be though, not if Charlotte could help it.

"I'm sure she'll be back to herself in no time," Mary was saying as she steered her away.

Charlotte suspected she was the only one who heard the wry amusement in Mary's tone. She ignored it, whispering to her friend that she'd explain everything when they were alone.

It would be all right. It had to be. She wasn't certain how she would have a word with Lord Thomas now. Nor how she could ascertain her parents' acceptance of Lord Paul even if Lord Thomas was out of the picture.

But with the feel of Paul's kiss still stinging her lips, she found herself grinning as she let Mary lead her to her bedroom.

There was still much to work out but only one thing of which she was truly certain. This was fate.

It was destiny.

Nothing in the world could come between her and Paul now. Not her parents. Not his family.

And certainly not the dreadfully dull Lord Thomas.

CHAPTER TEN

Thomas's head was spinning when he rejoined the guests in the ballroom.

"Well?" Paul asked, coming to join him in a corner near the refreshments the moment he stood still. "How did it go?"

"I'm still trying to figure out what happened," Thomas said.

This was not a lie, nor even an evasion. He truly was trying to understand.

She still didn't know. How did she *not* know? She'd asked to see Lord Thomas and he'd arrived. The crush of guests around him was making it impossible to think clearly. Thomas headed toward a wall and leaned against it, taking a deep steadying breath.

Paul stood beside him but leaned forward, craning his neck. His face drew so close to Thomas's that Thomas shoved him away. "What are you doing?"

Paul smirked. "Just trying to find the bruises. She must have thrown something at your head. What was it? A book? Libraries have loads of those, or so I hear."

Thomas shook his head, ignoring his friend's jests. "This isn't funny," he bit out.

"Says you," Paul said. "From where I'm standing, this entire ordeal is ridiculous and absurd and I'm dying to catch the conclusion of this farce."

Thomas pinched the bridge of his nose with a sigh of exasperation.

"So?" Paul prompted. "How did it go over when you told her?"

A silence passed before Thomas admitted the horrible truth. "I didn't."

Another silence. "What do you mean, you didn't?"

"I thought..." Thomas dropped his hand and cleared his throat, as he realized the full extent of his own idiotic assumptions. "I thought she knew that I was Lord Thomas coming to meet her."

Paul stared at him in clear disbelief.

Truthfully, he was having a difficult time believing himself. He replayed her words, her expression.

It's you, she'd cried.

He'd thought she'd meant 'it's you' as in 'you are Lord Thomas.'

He raked a hand through his hair, mussing the neatly slicked style his butler had taken such pains to exact.

"Paul, what will I do?" he asked.

His friend shook his head. "What you ought to have done from the beginning, I'd imagine." He gripped his shoulders and gave him a well-deserved shake. "Tell the girl who you are."

He nodded. Right. Of course. He just had to do so before she found out from someone else.

"Thomas, there you are," his father said.

Thomas stiffened and shared a wary look with Paul before

they both turned to face his father, who looked more unpleasant than usual. No doubt because he was wasting his evening at a ball when he had work to do or a gentleman's club to visit.

His father was rarely a happy man, and seemed to forever be put out by wherever he was. The man was mulishly intent on being unhappy no matter the fact that he'd been blessed with power and wealth that most men couldn't even dream of.

"Where have you been?" his father snapped, his voice too low to draw attention but loud enough that Paul cringed beside him in sympathy.

"I've been right here, Father." He adopted the bored tone he'd learned how to emulate years ago. "Was there something you needed?"

His father's ruddy cheeks grew red with fury. "I need you to stop being such a useless, lazy knave and do the one job you've been tasked with."

Thomas opened his mouth to remind his father that they were in public, but it was too late. His father was already off on another set down that left Thomas's insides flayed while his expression and bearing did not falter.

To show any sign of emotion in front of his father was akin to airing a weakness. It was not taken to kindly and only made matters worse.

"...that's all you've been put on this earth for, you hopeless excuse for a son. And now you've gone and made me look like a fool in front of Meagher and his son. Is that what you wanted?"

"No, sir," he said stiffly.

Passersby were slowing their pace to catch some of what his father was muttering, but fortunately Paul was doing a fine job of casting withering glares at anyone who might think to linger.

Thomas's pride would remain intact, at least. And he would not be broken by this man. Not today, not ever.

His mother joined them, her eyes cast down and her gaze distant as if she could not hear her husband's insults.

Perhaps she couldn't. It would explain how she'd survived this long in a marriage to the cruel, angry old goat.

"Your mother tried to find you," his father continued. As if he were angry on his wife's behalf.

As if he cared one whit about the feelings of anyone besides himself. "She was trying to find you so you might be introduced to your wife—"

"She's not my wife yet," he bit out. He couldn't stop himself.

He didn't want his father speaking of Charlotte. He didn't want him talking of her as if she were his to command.

She wasn't. She never would be.

Charlotte deserved so much better than a man like this.

I will not marry Lord Thomas, no matter what they promise.

His stomach twisted in revulsion as he watched spittle fly from his father's mouth, his eyes hard and cold.

This was the sort of man she thought him to be. And tonight had been his best chance to explain himself to her, and he'd missed it. Again.

How could she not have realized that he was Lord Thomas?

But then again...

If one sees the world one particular way, perhaps it was all too easy to color everything with that hue.

Yes, the more he thought on it, the more he could understand her confusion. She'd thought he knew she'd be there and had beaten Lord Thomas to the meeting spot. She'd thought...

Oh blast. He didn't know what she'd thought. He stared blankly at his father as his mind spun.

What had she meant then when she'd said she'd heard all about him and his childhood? Confusion muddled his mind and made him deaf to his father's blustering.

He's assumed she'd meant Lord Thomas. It had made sense that her family would have regaled her with stories about her fiancé.

He glanced over at Paul.

Why would she know anything about Paul?

It made no sense.

The sudden quiet around him jarred him back to the moment and he realized his father was subdued enough now as he listened to Thomas's mother speak quietly.

"Yes, yes. That's what he'll have to do," his father said. "We can't keep allowing Thomas to ruin our well-laid plans."

The way Paul's stare had turned to a wary wince had Thomas blinking rapidly to clear his mind and focus on what was being said around him.

"What is?" he interjected.

Both of his parents turned to him as if surprised he might be taking an interest in his own life, which was clearly being discussed without his input.

His mother's brows arched in question and he took pains to keep his voice even as he said, "What is it I must do to keep from ruining your plans?"

"We'll make the agreement official tonight," his mother said simply. "It's a simple matter of working out the details, anyhow."

"Simple. Nothing is simple when your son tries his best to shirk his duties at every turn," his father muttered.

Thomas's back was rigid, his muscles tensed. "Tonight?"

"We won't announce it just yet," his mother said in a tone he supposed was meant to sound soothing. "There will be time for that yet."

"You cannot—" He started and stopped abruptly, aware of

his father's glare and Paul's meaningful look warning him not to make the situation worse.

But it couldn't possibly get any worse.

He still needed to explain the misunderstanding to Charlotte. He couldn't let her find out like this. And she was dead set on not marrying Lord Thomas. Not marrying *him*. To force her tonight, before she knew the full truth...

It wasn't fair to her. And it wasn't right for her to be trapped in an agreement when she did not know the whole of it.

"We cannot," he said simply.

This was met with three stares of disbelief. Only his father's was tempered with fury. "What do you mean?"

"She does not even know me," he started, his tone soft and placating. Logical, he hoped. His father could sometimes be reasoned with using logic.

"She's wary of marriage, you said so yourself." He turned a somewhat accusatory gaze on his mother, who winced as if he'd slapped her.

"I merely meant..." She faltered when his father's withering glare turned to her. "She's young, that's all. Her parents will bring her around and she will see reason."

Like you did?

He couldn't bring himself to ask his mother if she'd ever fought the arranged marriage with his father. Had she even known him back then? Had she known the sort of man she'd be shackled to for the rest of her life?

Had she feared him before they'd even met or was this constant fear a learned state after the wedding?

Pity for his mother swelled in his chest, but it only made him more certain that he would not subject Charlotte to any such torture. He was not his father. He knew this well.

But she did not. Not yet.

"What does it matter what the girl wants?" his father's

brow was furrowed in clear confusion and disgust at the turn of this conversation. "She'll do as her father bids. Just as you will do as I command," he barked.

The crowd around them turned to look, and Thomas let out a sigh of gratitude when the pianoforte began to sound from the far side of the room.

Tonight's event was a small gathering as the season had not officially begun, but the room was still far too crowded for a conversation such as this one.

His father leaned in closer and lowered his voice so no one could overhear. "We will draw up the marriage contracts tonight, do you hear me? And if her father wishes to announce your engagement, then you will nod and smile and say all the pretty words expected of you—"

"But Miss Charlotte—"

"And Miss Charlotte will do as she is bid. She'll be yours to command soon enough, Son," he growled. "You'd best learn how to get her in hand."

His father's attention was called by a gentleman behind Thomas and his father's demeanor shifted from one of overbearing father to a congenial earl in the blink of an eye.

His mother watched him for a long moment after her husband walked away but she said nothing. Her eyes showed even less.

Finally, with a pat of his arm, she followed after his father and Thomas was left alone with Paul.

Paul sighed loudly in clear relief. "And I thought my father was difficult to manage."

They shared a wry, bitter laugh. The two spares and their fathers who loathed them. This was who they were and why they'd stayed such close friends despite the fact that they had nothing else in common.

It was why Paul knew enough to stand there in silence and leave Thomas to his thoughts. When the music came to an end, Paul turned to him with a cocked brow. "Well, old friend? What will you do?"

Thomas shook his head, but he knew. Deep down, he'd known from the start. "I cannot force her to marry me. I cannot be a party to her misery."

"But she likes you," Paul argued. "You said so yourself."

Thomas turned to his friend, his chest sinking in despair. Why had he not spoken bluntly for once? Instead, he'd let himself get swept away by romance and passion.

Why had he kissed her without speaking the words that could have put a simple end to her confusion?

I am Lord Thomas.

Was that so hard?

He scrubbed a hand over the back of his neck.

Apparently so.

"She cannot find out who I am like this," he said. "Not in front of our parents. And not while being told that the agreement is binding."

"So what will you do?" Paul asked, wariness lacing his voice.

Thomas sighed again. He hated this. But it was the only option. They could not force an introduction if he was not here to be introduced. "I'll have to leave her. I'll have to let her suffer through this night on her own."

CHAPTER ELEVEN

"Well, that *was* close," Mary breathed when they'd finally escaped through the crowded hallways and the music-laden drawing room to the private quarters beyond.

They'd only just entered Charlotte's bedroom when Mary swung around to face her. "Now. Tell me everything."

Her eyes were wide with curiosity and Charlotte couldn't help but laugh as she clasped her hands to her chest. "It was heavenly."

Mary's brows drew down. "So it went well then?"

Charlotte's head tipped back with a wistful sigh as she recalled the feel of Paul's lips on hers, the way he'd held her so tightly as if he'd never let go. "It went exceedingly well, Mary."

Mary's silence had Charlotte lifting her head once more to look at her friend.

Her friend who was now frowning, confusion pinching her pretty features. "So..." Mary cocked her head to the side. "Lord Thomas let you out of your agreement then?"

Now it was Charlotte's turn to frown in confusion. Mary

had been standing right there when Paul snuck out of the library. She'd seen him with her own eyes.

Mary arched her brows hopefully. "Did Lord Thomas say he will support your decision and break the news to your parents?"

Charlotte stared at her friend for a long moment. Odd. She'd always thought Mary so very clever, but today she seemed remarkably slow. "Mary, dear, perhaps you did not understand. Lord Thomas did not arrive for our rendezvous." She pursed her lips. "Or perhaps he did, but I was already otherwise engaged."

A smile tugged at her lips. *Otherwise engaged with kissing the man I love.*

Mary blinked. Then she blinked again. "I do not understand. If that was not Lord Thomas leaving the library, who was it?"

"What do you mean? Who was it?" Charlotte's voice was sharper than intended. Not in anger, but...fear. A gnawing, cloying fear was building in the pit of her stomach at the clear confusion in Mary's eyes.

Mary. The one person she knew who was actually acquainted with Lord Paul.

Mary, who hadn't so much as shared a glance of acknowledgement with Lord Paul when he'd slipped out of the library.

"Mary," she said slowly, a chill slithering down her spine and making her skin tighten and crawl.

"Yes?" Mary breathed, as if she too could feel the dawning horror.

Charlotte wet her lips. "You did see the gentleman slip out of the other library door, did you not?"

Mary nodded. "I did. And I assumed...that is..." She arched her brows. "Was that *not* Lord Thomas?"

"No, it was not." She swallowed hard. "That was Lord

Paul."

Mary stared at her in clear confusion.

"Wasn't it?" Charlotte's voice was pathetically small.

Mary shifted, her hands clasped before her. "I did not recognize the gentleman who'd slipped into the hallway."

Charlotte's breathing grew harsh. "Are you saying...?" Oh drat, her gown was far too tight and she couldn't properly draw in air.

How could a lady think when she couldn't even breathe?

She stumbled back and fell down onto her bed. "Mary, are you saying that was *not* Lord Paul?"

Mary winced and eyes filled with something shockingly close to pity. "Perhaps...perhaps there is another Lord Paul?"

Charlotte just stared at her friend. For the first time in her life, she was incapable of speech.

There was not another Lord Paul and they both knew it. Not one who'd have been picking up books for Lady Galena.

Her stomach lurched, her chest tightening so quickly she was certain her heart was being crushed in the process. Her hands fisted in the covers beneath her. "I...I don't understand."

Mary knelt before her, concern written all over her features as she reached for her hands.

"Mary," she said slowly. "If that was not Lord Paul leaving the library then...then who did I just kiss?"

Mary's eyes widened, but she had no answer.

A knock on her open door had Charlotte darting up off the bed and Mary climbing to her feet.

Eloise hovered in the doorway. "Pardon the intrusion," she said with a smile.

Charlotte wasn't capable of an answering smile. Her head was still spinning.

"Mother and Father wish to see you," Eloise said. "They're in Father's study with Lord and Lady Calloway."

Lord Thomas's parents. She gulped. This could only mean one thing. There was no reason her parents would wish for her to meet with Lord Thomas's family unless they were meant to discuss the impending engagement.

She couldn't become engaged tonight. She could not. Not after kissing another man.

Eloise and Mary were watching her closely. "Well?" Eloise said when she failed to move.

She'd kissed another man. And she didn't even know who he was.

Oh this could not be happening.

This was not her life.

"Come along," Eloise said with another encouraging smile. "They won't wish to be kept waiting."

Charlotte's feet moved haltingly as if of their own accord. But really, what was the use in prolonging the inevitable. "Is Lord Thomas with them?"

Eloise shook her head. "Not yet. His father sent his friend to find him."

She stopped short in the middle of the room. "He's not here?"

Relief swept through her. For a second there she'd had the most horrible suspicion. But if Lord Thomas wasn't in attendance then of course it could not have been him.

"No," Eloise said. "Not at the moment, at least." She forced a bright smile. "Perhaps he's just stepped out for some fresh air." Charlotte's sister placed a hand on her arm and led her toward the door. "Don't fret. I'm sure he'll turn up. Lord Paul has promised to find him."

Charlotte stumbled over her own two feet. "Lord Paul?"

Eloise smiled. "Oh yes, he's Lord and Lady Galena's youngest son. A dear friend of Lord Thomas's, I've been told."

Charlotte turned back to see that Mary had gone deathly pale.

"I see," Charlotte said slowly, turning back and allowing Eloise to steer her down the hallway toward her father's study.

Her mind had gone blank now, too overwhelmed to make sense of it all.

"When did Lord Thomas leave?" Mary asked from behind her.

Clever, clever Mary. She never should have doubted her friend.

"I don't know. It's odd, really." Eloise frowned. "He was here earlier. I can't imagine where he might have gone."

"He was here earlier," Charlotte repeated like a simpleton. "You know this," she added slowly. "Because...because you spoke to Lord Thomas."

"Of course." Eloise gave her a small, knowing smile. "I spoke to him on your behalf, as you may recall." She turned to face her fully, a crease forming above the bridge of her nose. "How did that go? Was he understanding of your hesitations? Was he...?" Eloise bit her lip. "Was he kind?"

They all stopped walking now, the sounds of the revelries taking place in the common areas below jarringly at odds with Eloise's somber tone.

Was he kind?

All at once Charlotte saw *him* in her mind's eye. The tender affection in his eyes. The smile that tugged at his lips. "Yes," Charlotte found herself saying. "He was kind."

Eloise breathed out a sigh of relief. "That is a relief. I know he looks stern and formidable, but I thought I saw kindness in his eyes."

"He does look rather stern, doesn't he?" Charlotte said. Her heart raced and her stomach pitched as understanding dawned. "How else would you describe him?"

Eloise arched her brows and Mary made a strangled sound behind her.

"What do you mean?" Eloise said.

Mary leapt in. "The library was so dark," she explained. "I don't believe Charlotte managed to get a good look at Lord Thomas."

Charlotte cast her friend a quick look. It *was* Lord Thomas, Mary thought so too.

Eloise nodded as if this made sense. "Well, he has light brown hair. Nearly blond, I'd say. And like I said, his features are rather forbidding. Not one to smile or laugh often, I'd say..."

Eloise continued, and with each word about his height and breadth, his manner of speaking, and the way he held himself, she drew a vivid picture of him.

Her Lord Paul. Who, of course, was not really Lord Paul at all.

A fact that was made appalling clear when a tall, dark-haired gentleman with bright blue eyes and a hawkish nose turned the corner as if he too were heading for the study. He nearly collided with them in his haste.

"Oh," he said as he stopped short, his gaze taking in all three of them. "My apologies. I did not see you there, Miss Haverford," he said to Eloise. His gaze slid past her to Charlotte before landing on Mary. His eyes widened slightly. "Miss Mary. I did not expect to see you here."

"Lord Paul," Mary said in a bland tone by way of greeting.

His answering smirk was far from kind.

And Charlotte's world officially tipped upside down.

"I wasn't aware they let you off the farm," Lord Paul said to Mary.

"It's not a farm," she snapped.

Eloise looked to Mary in surprise, but Lord Paul was chuckling as if this was a longstanding joke. "If you'll excuse me, ladies, I'm meant to report back to Lord Calloway." His gaze slid to Charlotte briefly before he turned away.

The look was brief, but telling.

There was pity there, she was sure of it. Or at least sympathy.

He knew. He knew that his friend had deceived her.

Anger fizzled in her blood and for a moment it was hard to hear past the roar of blood in her ears.

Lord Thomas had tricked her.

Her hearing returned just in time for her to catch her father's booming voice ringing out from within the study. "What do you mean you cannot find him?"

Her brother's voice was next, calmer and gentler as he tried to keep the peace, as always. "I'm sure he'll turn up, Father."

An unfamiliar male voice joined the mix, calm and cold enough to make Charlotte shiver. "You know how young men can be, Meagher," he said to her father. "My son has agreed to the match and I can speak on his behalf as far as the contract goes."

Her head felt light and she was dimly aware that her sister and Mary were standing on either side of her now, their arms wrapped around her.

That was when she realized she'd been swaying.

Charlotte clenched her hands into fists at her side. She'd never been the type to faint, and she surely would not start now.

But the conversation continued, and much as Eloise tried to steer her away, she could not bring herself to leave.

"Your son is not going to try and cry off once we've made this official, is he?" her father demanded. "I will not abide having our family name tarnished just because your son is not keen on marriage. His actions thus far have made it abundantly clear he doesn't wish to marry our Charlotte—"

"He'll do as he's told," Lord Calloway said, his voice firm.

Charlotte felt as if she'd been slapped. She could still feel the heat of his lips pressed to hers, hear the low sound of his promises in her ears...

But no. He hadn't made any promises. Not really.

Her father's words rang in her ears.

He didn't want to marry her.

His father was still speaking, his voice that of a commander on a battlefield rather than a gentleman discussing his son's forthcoming marriage. "Make no doubt about it, Meagher. Thomas might not be happy about marrying your daughter, but he understands his duty."

The conversation continued, and her sister and Mary kept trying to tug her away. They clearly didn't want her to hear anymore, but it was too late.

She'd heard enough. It was all becoming clear. So horribly, awfully clear.

"They haven't even been introduced," a soft female voice said. It must have been Lord Thomas's mother. "Perhaps we should wait—"

"We've waited long enough," Lord Calloway said.

Even Eloise and Mary flinched at his angry boom.

"We'll not leave it to children to decide when there's so much at stake," his father continued.

Her mother's voice joined in the mix, soothing and reasonable. "They will be introduced in time and grow to appreciate one another," she said. "Lord Calloway is right. It is time to finalize the arrangement. Our children know their duty."

Finally, Charlotte could fight it no longer. Her sister and Mary were pushing her back toward her bedroom. No one seemed to have noticed that she'd never arrived though she'd been summoned.

Her parents required her presence for this conversation just as little as they needed Lord Thomas's input.

She was only dimly aware of Mary's arm around her when they once more sank down on the edge of the bed, and she only caught bits and pieces of Eloise's reassuring words about how it would all be all right in the end.

"They were wrong, though," Charlotte finally said when she lifted her head. Her eyes were filled with tears and her heart ached. Not because her engagement would soon be official but because the man she'd thought she loved was a liar and a fake.

"Wrong?" Eloise said, her brows arched in question.

She turned to see Mary frowning with concern.

"We have met," she said slowly, her heart sinking with each word. "At least, he has met me."

He'd wanted to get to know his new bride. That much she could understand. She couldn't even have said she wouldn't have done the same if the situations were reversed. He'd wanted to know what sort of woman he was getting and so he'd let her believe he was someone else. He'd encouraged her to be herself.

Her heart twisted painfully in her chest.

His duplicity stung. The fact that she did not know how much of the Lord Thomas she'd come to know was an act made her belly twist and roil.

But what really made her feel as though her heart might break in two...?

"He met me," she said slowly. "And yet tonight he left."

Thomas might not be happy about marrying your daughter, but he understands his duty. His father's words came back to her like a knife in the gut.

"He left because he met me. The real me." Her voice shook. "And he does not want me."

CHAPTER TWELVE

Thomas's mother stood stiff and straight beside him as they waited outside the School of Charm.

"You cannot put this off any longer," his mother said quietly.

"I know."

"Neither can she," she added.

He nodded. He knew that too, but it didn't stop his insides from rebelling at the thought. He'd been livid with his parents when they'd woken him the next day with the news that he was now engaged to marry Charlotte.

He was a man. A grown man at that.

Then start acting like it, his father had shouted back.

A full on shouting match, that was what had occurred. For the first time since he was a child Thomas had dropped the act that he was as cool and unfeeling as his father. He'd ranted and raved, his emotions on full display, much to his father's horror. But in the end, what had it gotten him?

Thomas could back out of the agreement. It wasn't his father's right to promise him to anyone. But to do so would only hurt Charlotte.

Her reputation, at least.

Would she thank him if he set her free? Or would she hate him even more than she likely already did?

The door opened and a housekeeper welcomed them inside. "Lady Meagher, Miss Farthington, and Miss Charlotte will join you momentarily," she said as she led them into a small but well-appointed drawing room.

In the distance he heard muffled voices, but the drawing room was silent. His mother took a seat on the settee, but nerves and anticipation of Charlotte's reaction upon seeing him made it impossible for him to stand still, let alone sit.

He paced the length of the room under his mother's watchful eye.

She'd been present for the argument this morning. Now she no doubt worried that he'd run off again, as he had the night before.

His normally kind, if distant mother had given him a look of such disappointment this morning that he still couldn't quite meet her gaze. She didn't have to tell him she'd thought his actions callous and weak.

Of course, she had. To her, and everyone else involved, it had no doubt seemed as though he'd jilted his bride-to-be before he'd even met her.

Was that what Charlotte had thought?

Useless ponderings. All last night and even during a fitful sleep, his thoughts had been filled with these questions. What did she think of him? Of Lord Thomas and Lord Paul?

Did she know that the agreement had been finalized?

Was she waiting for him to come save her and take her away?

He eyed the door warily. Would she faint or scream when she caught sight of him here and realized the truth of his identity?

He had no idea what to expect. And when at last the door

opened and a petite brunette entered, followed by Lady Meagher, and then at last by Charlotte, he knew with utmost certainty that he never would have expected *this.*

Charlotte smiled brightly at him as they were introduced, her eyes wide and eager. "How do you do?" she said prettily as she curtsied under her mother's watchful gaze.

She did not seem surprised at all.

In fact...

His stomach sank as she lifted her head and her eyes met his. She didn't seem to be feeling *anything* at all. While her smile was bright and her tone light and charming, her eyes were empty. Vacant.

They were also missing something.

Where are your spectacles? He almost blurted it out but stopped himself just in time.

His mother and hers filled the air with words. Lots of words. Words that might as well have been gibberish for all the meaning they conveyed.

All the while he tried his best to get Charlotte to look at him. No, that wasn't right. She was looking at him, but she wasn't seeing him. And it wasn't because of her lack of spectacles either. Although he was a bit alarmed when she was tasked with pouring tea and nearly missed the cup.

Why wasn't she wearing her spectacles?

And why was she smiling like that?

When his mother turned to her and asked her how she was liking her new school and how she was adapting to being back in London, her answers made him even more alarmed.

"I like it very much, Lady Calloway," she said sweetly.

Too sweetly. What she said wasn't the alarming part, but rather the way she said it. He barely recognized her voice; it was so quiet, and even, and prim and proper.

There was not so much as a hint of the lively, vivacious ray of sunshine he'd come to know.

He sat across from Charlotte, but he might as well have been taking tea with a complete stranger.

Not that he was any better. Uncomfortable and ill at ease, he barely spoke at all. Which was not uncommon as far as his mother was concerned, but it felt odd to sit there so serious and grim while Charlotte was in his presence.

She'd taught him to smile. She'd made his laugh feel normal and real. She'd...

Oh curse it.

She'd made him feel like *himself,* and now he had no idea who he was anymore.

"More tea, Lord Thomas?" she asked sweetly.

So sweetly it made his teeth ache.

"No. Thank you."

Her smile broadened as if he'd said something clever. "Of course, my lord."

And that was how it continued for the longest hour of his life. *Yes, my lord. Of course, my lord. As you say, my lord.*

She was agreeable to a fault. Sweet to the nth degree.

It was maddening.

And he suspected she knew it. Just as he was now certain she'd known that it would be him showing up here today for this nightmare of a visit.

How had she discovered the truth?

Did it matter? Likely not. What mattered was that he find a chance to explain. Finding an opportunity proved difficult as she clearly had an ally in Miss Farthington. Each time their mothers were engaged in a private conversation and he'd attempt to lean in toward her for a word, Miss Farthington would interject with a question for him or a random remark about the weather for her.

He found himself scowling at Miss Farthington after the

fourth such interruption, even though the headmistress seemed nice enough. When she returned his scowl with an impish grin, his suspicions were confirmed.

Charlotte had asked her to intervene.

She was ensuring that she would not have to interact with him. Even though she *was* interacting, she wasn't. Not really.

He knew it. She knew it.

What was more, she knew that he knew it.

It wasn't until their visit was ending that the mothers touched on the topic of a wedding.

Their wedding.

That was the first moment he caught a chink in her armor. A flicker of emotion broke through the mask she'd been wearing. The perfect young lady. The happy bride to be. That was the role she'd been playing, and she'd been doing it well. If he hadn't been watching her so closely he might have missed the way her lips pinched and her nostrils flared.

That hint of emotion broke his heart.

She was hurting. And he'd been the one to hurt her. Desperation had him turning to the mothers and rudely interrupting. "Would it be all right if I escorted Miss Charlotte for a turn around the room?"

Her mother's face brightened. His mother's eyes narrowed in thought. But both were in agreement that this was a wonderful idea.

Neither asked for Miss Charlotte's opinion on the matter.

And indeed, she was once more smiling sweetly when he rose, strode toward her chair, and offered his arm.

"Are you enjoying this fine weather, my lord?" she asked when they were a few steps away, her voice so not like her own it gave him a chill.

"Lottie," he started.

He stopped abruptly when she shot him a sidelong glare.

"Miss Charlotte," he tried again.

"The streets were so crowded the other day when my mother and I were shopping. Have you noticed the same, my lord?" Her smile was back. More of a simper really, and her gaze cut right through him as if he were made of glass.

He'd like to think she just couldn't see him properly without her spectacles, but he doubted that was the case. She didn't wish to see him.

"Please, allow me to explain," he said in a low, urgent voice.

They'd reached the far side of the room and this was his opportunity to speak plainly.

"Explain what, Lord Thomas?" She batted her eyelashes as her vacant gaze looked through him. She did not give him a chance to speak. "I do apologize it has taken so long for us to meet. My health, you know. I'm afraid I've inherited my mother's nervous temperament."

He stopped short with a huff of exasperation. "You and I both know that is a lie, Lottie."

She pinched her lips together, still facing straight ahead with her chin held high.

The other ladies were watching them as they talked amongst themselves. A fact Charlotte seemed to be well aware of because she kept her expression neutral, even managing a small curve of her lips as she murmured, "How long?"

His chest tightened to hear her speaking normally. His heart ratcheted up into his throat. "I did not mean to fool you. You must believe me."

"Must I?" She turned to face him fully, and finally—*finally*—she looked directly at him.

He flinched at the anger he saw there, but it was the hurt that lingered beneath her ire that had his insides sinking.

"I promise you, Lottie, I never meant to hurt you."

"But you did," she shot back quickly. "You made a fool of me."

"No," he said. "I never intended—"

"Very well, then I made a fool of myself," she said. "I'd so wanted to believe—" She cut herself off with another pinch of her lips, her gaze darting past him as she started to walk again.

"What is it? What did you wish to believe?"

Her expression went frighteningly blank. "It does not matter. I've been acting like a child just like my family has always accused me of doing, but I am done with that now."

"Lottie—"

"It is Miss Charlotte," she said evenly. "Or Charlotte to you, I suppose, as we are to be married."

"Please believe me that I never set out to trick you," he said. "And I tried to explain—"

She cut him off with another piercing glare that left him tongue-tied.

Blast. She was right even if she hadn't outright said it. He hadn't tried hard enough. But that was only because he'd wanted to believe too. He'd been desperate to believe that there might be someone out there who truly saw him, and who loved him all the same.

He stopped suddenly. Was that what she'd been about to say?

His heart slammed against the walls of his chest as he turned to her. "I am sorry, Charlotte. Truly. And you must know—"

"'Twas a pity you two did not meet at the masquerade, Lord Thomas," her mother called out. "Our Charlotte looked quite lovely."

"I'm certain she did," he said.

He ignored Charlotte's quiet scoff. They were drawing too close to the others to say much more.

He'd apologized, at least. That was something. It was a start. Now if only he could find a moment alone to truly speak with her.

"You *were* beautiful that night," he said in a low voice, under his breath.

"My mother wasn't even there," Charlotte said in a rueful tone in a similarly soft voice.

He wasn't certain she'd heard him.

"You're always beautiful," he said.

"It truly was a pity we did not meet that night," she continued as if he hadn't spoken.

"Charlotte—"

"Instead, I met the most remarkable man," she said, her voice faint and dreamy.

His heart tripped and tugged.

They'd reached the others and she smiled up at him sweetly. Insincerely. "Unfortunately, I've come to discover he only exists in my imagination."

"Charlotte," he growled.

"Come along, Thomas," his mother said as she came to stand. "We have stayed too long as it is. I'm certain your Miss Charlotte has other social calls on her agenda today."

Charlotte was back to simpering again, her gaze so dazed she looked like an empty-headed simpleton. A fact he knew was not true.

Imaginative, yes. A bit naive? Perhaps. A romantic, of course. But she was not simple, nor was she dull.

She was just hiding, tucking away those parts of herself that she feared no one would ever appreciate.

He understood it well because he'd spent the better part of a lifetime doing the same.

He cast one last pleading look her way before following his mother. It wasn't until they were in the carriage and heading back home that his mother spoke. "I think that went well, don't you?"

He stared at her blankly. She could not be serious.

She gave him a small smile in response. "You two have a lifetime to get to know each other and to find some commonalities."

He grunted in response, turning to look out the window. He didn't need a lifetime to know she was the perfect woman for him. He was well aware.

No, he just needed to find a way to convince her to give him another chance.

"Let her get to know you, Thomas." His mother's voice was surprisingly gentle. "She will come to love you."

The words hit a nerve and he flinched. "Like you love father?"

She gave him a small smile again, one that said she understood precisely what he was doing. "You are not your father."

Thank heavens.

The words went unspoken between them as they so often did.

"Perhaps it's time you stop pretending you are," she added softly.

He jerked back in his seat, his gaze darting over to meet hers. "I don't...I'm not..." He let out a huff of irritation because he knew what she meant. He'd learned to evade his father's disdain and displeasure by imitating him, pretending to be just like the stern, formidable man. Easy enough to do since they shared the same hard features and gruff voice.

But he wasn't his father. A fact few ever realized.

But Charlotte had.

He swallowed hard and looked back out the window. "I don't know how to get to know her. Or to let her know me."

Not as himself. Not with others watching.

Not while having to play the part he'd created for himself.

A long silence passed before his mother spoke again. "I think what the two of you need is some time alone—"

He shot her an arch look and she blushed.

"Not *that* alone. But away from your father and her mother and somewhere you might both be more comfortable."

He stared at her evenly as he waited for her to continue. His heart was starting to race again, this time with new hope. Maybe even anticipation. "What did you have in mind?"

CHAPTER THIRTEEN

Miss Farthington poked her head into Charlotte's room. "Am I interrupting?"

"Not at all," Charlotte said.

Indeed, she was certain at least one person in this room was grateful for the interruption.

Miss Lydia Forsythe had arrived only this morning to the School of Charm and she'd yet to say more than two words, and nothing above a whisper. The shy girl was slight and frail and had honey-brown hair that was currently piled atop her head.

"We were just asking Miss Lydia about her travels," Mary said to Miss Farthington.

Miss Farthington took in Miss Lydia's pink cheeks and dipped head with a gentle, maternal smile. "Miss Lydia, your maid has finished unpacking your belongings if you'd like to retire to your room and rest until dinnertime."

The girl was on her feet and hurrying toward the door with a polite murmur so quiet, Charlotte couldn't actually make out the words.

When she closed the door shut with a click behind her, Charlotte turned to Miss Farthington with arched brows. "Your new pupil is as quiet as a mouse, isn't she?"

"She's certainly shy," Miss Farthington laughed. "I believe that is precisely why she's here. I'm hoping I can help the poor, timid lady come out of her shell."

"We shall help in any way we can," Mary said.

Charlotte nodded her agreement. She'd been cursed with many unwanted traits—at least, unwanted by her family—but fortunately timidity had never been one of them.

"Thank you," Miss Farthington said, but her gaze was already returning to Charlotte, and her hesitant expression had Charlotte bracing.

"What is it?" she asked.

Mary came to her side to take her hand as Miss Farthington held out a letter.

Charlotte looked closer. No, not a letter...

"An invitation," Mary said as she read over Charlotte's shoulder.

Miss Farthington nodded. "Lady Calloway has requested that we join her and her son at their home in the country."

Her gaze was fixed on Charlotte.

Charlotte swallowed hard, her belly aflutter at the mention of Thomas. Only two days had passed since that dreadful meeting with her betrothed and she still wasn't certain how she felt about it. Or him.

Her gaze lingered on the invitation. It had been written in Lady Calloway's hand, of course. She was now intimately familiar with Lord Thomas's after having reread and analyzed his every missive for some sort of hint. Some clue as to what he'd been thinking. What he'd been planning...

"The invitation is for all of us," she said quietly.

What did that mean? Was this house party Lady Calloway's idea or her son's?

Did it matter?

She pursed her lips. If only she had an answer. Any one would do. Not for the first time since she'd said her farewell to Lord Thomas the other day, Charlotte was regretting her stubborn pride. She'd been so determined to ignore her fiancé, to shut him out with coldness and keep him at bay with propriety.

She'd done a decent job of it. He'd been the one caught off guard for once, and for a little while that had given her satisfaction.

But now...

Well, by not allowing him to say his piece, she'd stolen her own chance at hearing his explanation.

The silence in the room grew as she stared unseeingly now at the invitation in her hands.

Mary and Miss Farthington had been so kind about not prying since Lord Thomas's visit. Well, Miss Farthington had not pried. Mary had asked plenty of questions but took Charlotte's answering silence without insult.

She seemed to understand that Charlotte wasn't certain what to make of her new fiancé just yet.

Charlotte toyed with the parchment in her hands as she studied his mother's fine script.

She likely would not know what to make of Lord Thomas until she'd had more of a chance to get to know him.

But the thought made her belly twist and turn with fear.

She drew in a sharp inhale, her gaze lifting to meet Miss Farthington's. "Do you think I should go?"

"That is entirely up to you, dear," the headmistress said. "But if it were me and this was my future at stake..." She pressed her lips together and met Charlotte's gaze evenly. "Charlotte, you do not strike me as the sort to shy away from anything, not even something that frightens you."

Charlotte's lower lip trembled. She wasn't one to cower in fear. But that was precisely what this was. Fear.

"What if he's not the man I thought him to be?" she asked.

Miss Farthington did not know the whole of the story. The sweet, clever woman had been content with the altered story that Charlotte had told her. But she understood enough.

"Oh, my dear," she said with a sigh as she reached for Charlotte's free hand.

Mary still clung to the other and between them Charlotte felt like a wishbone about to be snapped in two.

But while Miss Farthington's expression was sympathetic, of course she did not have the answer.

"I am trapped," Charlotte said to her two dear friends. "I am trapped with him for life either way."

"So then..." Mary hesitated, her brow furrowed in thought. "Wouldn't you rather know who he is? The real Lord Thomas, I mean?"

Charlotte bit her lip. "I suppose I am afraid to find out." She shrugged. "It is not as though I can end the engagement, now can I?"

She glanced to Miss Farthington hurriedly. "Oh, I am sorry," she said softly. "I did not mean—"

"No, no. Think nothing of it," Miss Farthington responded with a smile. She patted Charlotte's hand gently. "I do not regret for a moment that my own engagement came to an end, but I would not wish the repercussions on you. Not if you have any chance of finding happiness with that young man."

Charlotte and Mary exchanged a quick look. Little was known about Miss Farthington's former engagement or how it ended. All anyone truly knew was that Miss Farthington was the source of much gossip in the aftermath, which was how she'd come to be here at the school rather than out in society looking for a suitor of her own.

But looking at Miss Farthington now, she did not see a woman who was to be pitied. Not in the least. Standing here smiling, being a true friend and confidant to herself, Mary, and now that sweet, nervous creature who'd just arrived, their headmistress was the very picture of strength and courage.

If Miss Farthington could face her own whiff of scandal with a smile and her head held high, then surely Charlotte could withstand a conversation with her fiancé.

"I suppose I cannot avoid him forever," she said.

Though she had done a wonderful job of avoiding him the past two days when he'd arrived during visiting hours. Miss Farthington was nothing if not understanding when it came to Charlotte's sudden and debilitating megrims that left her indisposed.

"As his mother has invited all of us," Mary said, her gaze still on the invitation in Charlotte's hand. "We shall all be there to offer our support no matter how this goes."

Miss Farthington nodded. "Perhaps I can even convince Miss Lydia to join us for this outing." Her eyes sparkled with laughter. "We shall help you both overcome your fears."

Charlotte gave a decisive nod. "You are right. There's nothing to be gained by avoiding the inevitable."

A few days later, that newfound decisive confidence was nowhere to be found as her stomach lurched and roiled with each bump of the carriage.

Poor Miss Lydia looked to be just as ill at ease across from her, her face pale and her hands clenched together tightly. Only Mary and Miss Farthington seemed unfazed by the rocking of the carriage or their imminent arrival as they chatted and laughed, keeping the atmosphere in the carriage light as they made their way to Tomely Hall.

Despite the snow still on the ground, the sun was high overhead when they arrived, and the wind was brisk but not frigid.

Lord Thomas and his mother were waiting to greet them upon their arrival. Charlotte felt his eyes on her when she descended from the carriage, but she kept her gaze averted.

She felt like a coward.

She *was* a coward. But it was difficult to look at him and not remember the way he'd kissed her, the way he'd held her, the way he'd talked and laughed and—

And he'd certainly laughed, all right.

She straightened and turned away from his gaze. He must have laughed himself sick as she carried on about her dreams to run off with him.

Such a fool.

"My sister is here as well to act as chaperone," Lady Calloway was saying as they entered the stately home with its marble floors and dark-wood arches.

The home was lovely, but cold.

Like her parents' townhouse in London, the manor was elegant but not welcoming. Not at all like her Great Aunt Ida's home, which was far from fashionable but filled with laughter and warmth.

"Welcome, Miss Charlotte," Lord Thomas said when she could no longer avoid greeting him.

"Thank you for having us, my lord," she murmured in response.

His hand held hers and even through her glove she could feel his heat. Standing this close, she could smell his familiar scent and her insides went wild at his proximity.

She risked a glance up and nearly fainted dead away at the intensity in his eyes. There was no laughter there. Not at her expense. Not at all.

Her heart tried to soar and free fall all at once with that glimpse of his dark eyes. She was grateful he wasn't mocking her, of course. But it seemed a shame to see those eyes so flat and dull when they glinted so enchantingly when he was happy.

Had that been real? She wished she could ask. Was any of it real?

But his mother was joining them, welcoming her graciously along with the others, and Charlotte took the opportunity to tug her hand from Thomas's grip.

"Miss Charlotte," he said.

She glanced up and her breath caught at the fire in his eyes. She looked back down again, her skin burning under his watchful gaze.

"I hope we will have an opportunity to get to know one another better while you are here," he said quietly, for her ears only.

She nodded. "I would like that."

Her voice came out far too weak and she inwardly winced. She didn't sound like she'd meant it. But what was worse...

She wasn't certain if she'd meant it or not.

Oh, this was dreadfully confusing.

Lady Calloway led them to the drawing room for refreshments as the servants unpacked their trunks, and Charlotte, who'd been walking behind Mary, nearly stumbled right into her friend when Mary stopped short just inside the doorway.

"Oof! Mary?" she asked when her friend continued to block her path in the doorway. "What is it?"

Mary moved again, letting Charlotte come to her side inside the spacious, ornate drawing room. Her friend sighed wearily. "Rest assured, Lottie. You will not be the only one dreadfully uncomfortable during our stay."

For a moment Charlotte thought perhaps Mary was referring to shy little Lydia who looked as though she were trying to hide behind a potted plant in the corner. But then Charlotte followed Mary's gaze toward the small group that had already gathered on the far side of the room.

There was an older couple, a woman who must have been Lady Calloway's sister, and then...

"Oh dear," she murmured in sympathy.

"Indeed." Mary sighed again, this time with exasperation as Lord Paul looked over, caught Mary staring, and gave her a rakish wink.

"Will you be all right?" Charlotte asked.

Mary turned to her with a smile. "Of course. If you can manage to face Lord Thomas after all that's happened, then I can surely handle *him*."

The derision in her voice with that one word had Charlotte choking on a giggle. Just then she turned her head and found Thomas watching her. Again.

The smile still on her face started to fade, but then his lips twitched up, and for a moment, it was him again. Her Lord Paul.

Her gaze flickered over to the real Lord Paul. Oh drat. She'd have to stop thinking of him that way. It was getting far too confusing.

"Do you know," Mary said idly as they moved farther into the drawing room to join the others. "I believe we should blame Lord Paul for your fiancé's bad behavior."

Charlotte did laugh then, she couldn't help it. "And how is he to blame?"

Mary shot her a sidelong glance and an impish grin. "I do not know. But it seems the sort of mischievous prank that he would think up." She shrugged. "And they are friends, after all."

Charlotte laughed again as she linked arms with Mary.

"Something tells me you are just looking for an excuse to be annoyed with that handsome young man."

Mary scoffed and rolled her eyes. "Trust me, I have plenty of reasons to dislike Lord Paul. I don't need another."

"But you'll take one," Charlotte said after a beat.

Mary laughed. "Of course, I will."

CHAPTER FOURTEEN

Paul's voice was low and insistent beside him. "Now's your chance, old chum."

Thomas nodded. Their latest arrivals were spilling into the drawing room, but all he could see was Charlotte.

Her smile outshone every candelabra in this house—even if it dimmed slightly when she caught him staring.

Paul shifted closer. "Now, what you need to do is find a way to separate her from Miss Mary Contrary over there, and then pounce."

"Pounce?" Thomas tore his gaze away from Charlotte to glare at his friend. "We may be engaged but that does not give me the right to...to...to *pounce*."

Paul snickered. "You can stop looking so scandalized. I merely meant that if you can isolate her, maybe trap her alone somewhere, you'll finally be able to win her over."

Thomas scowled at this talk of isolation and trapping.

Paul returned his stare blankly. "What?"

"This is not a hunting expedition," Thomas said. "I merely mean to converse with my bride-to-be."

Paul scoffed. "Is that so? And here I thought you intended to woo the girl."

Thomas shifted, risking another glance in Charlotte's direction. "That too."

His heart hammered in his chest at the mere sight of her. He was relieved to see that she was wearing her spectacles today, and that fair sunlight-hued hair was wrapped around her head in a sort of braided crown. She wore a simple carriage dress, but the pale yellow only highlighted her rosy cheeks and sparkling eyes.

She was a vision. His lungs hitched.

And she was his.

"Why don't you listen to my advice?" Paul was saying. He clapped a hand on Thomas's shoulder. "You know I have a far better reputation when it comes to wooing the ladies, and—"

"And that is all well and good for you," Thomas said. "But Charlotte is not *some lady*. And besides, I'm done trying to pretend to be something I'm not."

His mother's words from the week before hadn't stopped playing in his mind. *You're not your father. Perhaps it's time you stop pretending you are.*

She'd made a valid point.

He'd grown so used to donning his father's demeanor that he sported that grim facade even now out of habit, like some well-worn old cloak that he'd long since outgrown.

That wasn't him any more than he could ever be an outgoing charmer like Lord Paul.

He was who he was. And like it or not, Charlotte was stuck with him. She ought to truly know him. And then she could decide once and for all if she wished to spend her life with him.

Paul acknowledged his words with a sigh. "All right, Thomas. How can I help?"

Thomas studied Charlotte for another long moment.

She'd gone back to whispering to her dark-haired friend while their headmistress and the other pupil stood talking to his mother and aunt. In addition, his mother had invited a few of her friends and he, of course, had asked Lord Paul to join for support.

There would likely be many opportunities to speak to Charlotte—after all, that was the entire reason his mother had set up this little winter house party.

That and to give them both some much needed distance from his father.

Things hadn't been the same between Thomas and his father since he'd summoned the nerve to stand up to the earl the other week regarding his high-handed actions in signing the marriage contract.

In fact, they'd had numerous arguments since. Not all as emotional nor fiery as the first, but those conversations had been enlightening, to say the least. He had a much better understanding now of the importance of his engagement in his father's eyes, and hers.

That was one of many topics he hoped to discuss with Charlotte during her stay. In private, of course.

His skin fairly itched with impatience to get her alone. The sight of her here had his heart aching as if it was calling out for her.

She'd agreed to come, and that was an excellent start. But until he properly explained himself, he could not imagine she was glad to see him.

Thomas turned back to Paul. "You were right in one regard. I do need to get her away from her friend."

"Indeed. Mary can ruin anyone's fun," Paul said.

Thomas shot his friend a questioning look. He'd never known Paul to be so rude about any young lady. Or any man either, for that matter. Though, judging by the smirk he wore, he was at least partially in jest.

"I shall keep Mary occupied," Paul said, his gaze frighteningly dark and fixed on the petite brunette as if he were the one with hunting in mind.

"Very well," Thomas said slowly. "Then I shall try to steal Charlotte away for a moment. The sooner I can explain myself to her the better."

Paul nodded. "And do you know what you will say?"

Thomas's mouth went dry and his throat grew choked. He'd had weeks now to sort through his thoughts and come up with an explanation, but he never had gotten the words right.

If only he could think of another way. His explanations sounded weak no matter what he said to his reflection in the mirror. And none of it was what Charlotte would wish to hear.

He might not have known Charlotte long, but he knew her well enough to know that she wouldn't take well to excuses and pleading. She'd want...

His mind raced.

She'd want laughter. She'd want passion. Something romantic and noteworthy, not just another weak attempt to rationalize his behavior.

She deserved something far more clever than he'd come up with to date.

"I don't know," he finally answered. "I do not know what to say. Truthfully, I don't wish to say anything at all."

Instantly his mind filled with the image of that kiss.

That was what he wanted. To show her how he felt. For a man so ill-disposed to words, that kiss was surely the most eloquent he'd ever been.

Paul gave a huff of amusement. "I think an explanation is still in order, I'm afraid to say."

"Yes, yes," Thomas said, waving a dismissive hand. "I

know that, of course. But I just wish..." He trailed off with a sigh.

"What?" Paul prompted.

"I just wish I could start over."

The statement hung in the air between them, and Thomas felt a buzzing in his mind with those words. A new idea was forming that had his heart racing and his palms sweating.

It just might work.

It would make her laugh, at least. And maybe, just maybe, she'd be willing to give him a second chance.

The only trouble was, how to arrange it?

His gaze snagged on her dark-haired friend. "Paul, what is it you have against Miss Mary?"

His friend chuckled. "You've got it wrong, old chum. It's not what I have against her. She's the one who despises me."

Thomas arched a brow and turned to his friend. "And so you dislike her because she dislikes you?"

He shrugged. "Well, when you put it like that, it sounds childish."

Thomas didn't respond. He let Paul's own words speak for themself.

"I think I should like a word with her first," Thomas said. Turning to his friend, he drew in a deep breath. "New plan. You distract Charlotte. I'll talk to Miss Mary."

"Me? With Charlotte?" Paul said, his eyes widening with shock. "And you and Mary?"

Thomas's brows arched at his friend's tone, not to mention the flush in his cheeks and the sudden snap of anger in his eyes when Paul said, "What do you want with Mary?"

Thomas blinked in surprise. "I just wish to have a word with her. I think I might have an idea for how to ensnare Charlotte."

He was already heading toward the two girls and ignored Paul's muttering behind him. "Ensnare her, eh?" Paul murmured. "And here I thought you weren't on a hunting expedition."

They'd joined Miss Mary and Charlotte before he could inform his friend that he was not on a hunting expedition.

It was more like...fishing.

He needed to lure her in because even now in the company of so many others, Charlotte was backing away from him, her gaze wary beneath the smile she'd plastered on.

He'd done this to her, whether it was intentional or not. He'd made her doubt him, and in turn he feared she doubted herself.

Her voice was still in his head from the last time he'd seen her. *I'd so wanted to believe,* she'd said.

He'd been wishing for a week now that she'd finished that thought. But he suspected he knew what she'd meant to say.

She'd thought that he cared for her. Just as she was.

He knew because he'd have felt the same.

He had felt the same, which was why it had been so difficult to come clean.

He forced himself to tear his gaze away from Charlotte's and turned his attention to Miss Mary instead. "Might I have a word?" he asked.

Mary blinked in surprise. Charlotte outright started.

Even Paul was eyeing him oddly, as if he'd lost his mind. But with a quick glance at Charlotte, Mary nodded and stepped away, allowing him to escort her to the windows where he made a show of gesturing to the grounds.

"...and over there is a grove of Aspen trees," he said as his heart hammered.

"Lovely," Mary murmured in response. Though her tone was low, bland, and utterly unimpressed. "Forgive the impertinence, my lord," she said as she turned to face him. "But was there some reason in particular you wished to speak to me?"

He cleared his throat. "Yes. Quite. You see..." He glanced past her and saw both Paul and Charlotte staring at him as they spoke to each other.

He turned his gaze to Mary. "I know I have no right to ask for favors—"

"Indeed, you do not," she said primly. "If you'll permit me to be blunt, my lord, you have done little to make me think your intentions are honorable."

He dipped his head. "You're right, of course. But I intend to make things right. With Charlotte, I mean. And while I know you do not owe me this favor, I'd still ask for your assistance."

"Why would I do that?" she asked.

He blinked in surprise. My, she was awfully forthright. He felt a smile tugging at his lips. "I can see why Charlotte is so fond of you, Miss Mary."

She tilted her head to the side, awaiting his response.

"I know I have made a mess of things," he said ruefully. "But my feelings for Charlotte are true. I want her to see this. To know this. And I believe the best way to her heart is by surprising her."

Mary blinked. "Surprising her? How? I should think getting engaged without her consent or even presence was surprising enough."

He flinched. "Er, yes. I meant more like a romantic gesture."

"Ah." She pinched her lips shut and narrowed her eyes to study him. He made no attempt to hide his desperation, nor his heart.

Whatever she saw, it had her smiling. "I do believe you are right."

He drew in a deep breath filled with relief.

"Now." She folded her hands neatly before her. "How can I help?"

CHAPTER FIFTEEN

Charlotte nearly tripped over her own feet as she allowed Mary to drag her down the empty hallway.

"Where are we going?" Charlotte asked.

Mary glanced over her shoulder with a grin. "I told you. I wish to see the library."

"Yes, but..." Charlotte stumbled. Goodness, Mary had a lively gait when she was excited about something. And apparently this evening she was excited about...books.

"You said yourself it would be great fun to explore this drafty old manor," Mary pointed out.

"Yes, but—eep!" She squeaked as Mary rounded a dark corner and nearly sent Charlotte colliding into a wall sconce.

"Must we explore tonight?" she asked. "They'll be calling us for dinner shortly."

Mary's glance took her in. "And you have been dressed and ready for an age. You should be grateful I am giving you a distraction before you put a hole in that fine rug in your room with your pacing."

Charlotte snickered. Her friend had a point.

She'd been beside herself with nerves ever since they'd

arrived. Her tension was made all the worse by Lord Thomas's odd behavior. Not to mention Mary's.

"You never did say what Lord Thomas spoke to you about," Charlotte said now as she gave in to Mary's tugs and let her lead the way down the darkened hall.

"Didn't I?" Mary was using the same vague, not at all helpful tone she'd been using for the last hour.

Charlotte huffed. "Fine. Then I suppose I must trust Lord Paul—"

"Nonsense." Mary stopped and spun to face her. "One should never trust Lord Paul."

"Yes, well, as Lord Paul was the only one to pay me any mind..." She trailed off meaningfully and Mary turned away again with a roll of her eyes.

"What did he say?" Mary asked.

"Not much," Charlotte said with a huff. "Just went on about what an upstanding fellow Lord Thomas is." She frowned. "But of course, he'd have to say that, wouldn't he? As his friend?"

"I don't know." Mary stopped and faced her with a small, rueful smile. "You are my friend and I have no problem admitting that you are a lunatic."

Charlotte choked on a laugh. "Mary!"

"It's true and you know it." Mary opened the door beside her and gave Charlotte a shove.

It was the library. Though how Mary was so certain of how to find it was a mystery.

Charlotte's insides tightened with foreboding. She'd been feeling as though Thomas and Mary were plotting somehow, and now she was sure of it. "Mary, what exactly are we here for?"

"Hmm? Oh. Oh no!" Mary did a terrible job of feigning shock. "I left my reticule in my room."

"But you do not need—"

"Be back in a jiffy," Mary said. "Why don't you explore without me for a moment."

"Explore—" Her echo was cut short as Mary closed the door shut behind her.

Charlotte was left alone. In silence. In the dark.

Well, not the *dark*-dark. There were candles lit. Almost as if...

Charlotte narrowed her eyes.

Almost as if she'd been expected.

She hovered there just inside the doorway with a frown as her eyes adjusted to the dim light. Floor to ceiling, there were books. So many books that her hands itched to skim over their binding and read the titles.

Would there be novels here?

No doubt. Lord Thomas might have lied about many things, but he'd held his own when talk had turned to literature.

She wet her lips and took another step inside the room. Then another. And then—

"Oof!" She cried out in surprise as the door was flung open behind her and a body careened into her. "What—? Who—?"

But she knew. She knew it the moment his arms closed around her to hold her steady. Knew it the second his scent enveloped her. Knew it the way his body pressed to hers felt like heaven on earth. Knew it in the way that his very presence here at her side felt like home.

All at once, the feelings she'd been trying to forget crushed her like an avalanche.

Thomas pulled back slightly, his arms still bracing her.

She tried to dip her head, but she was not quick enough.

"Don't cry, Lottie." He sounded so pained.

"I'm not." But she was and they both knew it.

A moment of silence passed before he cleared his throat,

his body straightening as if he'd come to some decision. "Are you all right?"

She nodded quickly. He hadn't hurt her. Not physically, at least. He'd just startled her. "Of course, I'm—"

"Then please," he interrupted quickly. Stepping back to put a proper distance between them while extending a hand. "Allow me to introduce myself."

She blinked. Her gaze dropped to his hand. "Um...what?"

She glanced up in time to see his throat work. But what was more, his eyes. They glinted. Maybe it was a trick of the candlelight, but...

She tilted her head to the side to study him, her breath catching in her throat.

His gaze met hers and he reached down to take her fingers in his, lifting the back of her gloved hand to his lips. "I am Lord Thomas, son of the Earl of Calloway."

A laugh bubbled up inside her as it became clear. The amusement in his eyes made sense now. But there was hesitation there too. Uncertainty at how she would respond.

She curtsied, her hand still in his. "Lord Thomas, what a pleasure," she breathed. Her heart was racing too quickly for her to catch up.

"And you are?" he prompted. His brows were arched but his lips quirked up, a hint of the smile she'd come to love.

"Miss Charlotte Haverford," she said quietly. "My parents are—"

"Why, you must be Lord Meagher's daughter," he exclaimed over top of her.

She just barely stifled a giggle. Or rather, a giggle and a sob. She hardly knew which would escape if she were to open her mouth.

He was doing this for her. Giving them a fresh start.

"I am," she said, going along with his act.

"Then you are the beautiful young lady I've heard so

much about over the years," he said. "The one my parents hope for me to marry."

"Yes, my lord," she said.

A silence fell as their gazes met. The heat in his made her heart feel like it was melting. She started to lean in toward him, her body drawn to his as if by gravity.

But then he pulled back with a start. "Well, now that the introductions are through, allow me to help you."

Charlotte blinked. 'Help me?"

He leaned down, pulling a book from behind his back as he did and pretending to pick it off the ground. "How clumsy of me. You must have dropped this when I so rudely collided with you."

Her eyes were so wet with tears she could only just barely make out the title as she took the book from him. *Frankenstein; or the Modern Prometheus.*

Of course.

"What's that?" Lord Thomas said a bit too loudly. He turned to look in the direction of an armchair. "Oh, no, no, Mr. Bookseller, I am afraid you are mistaken. I am not Lord Paul. I am merely here to fetch his order for his mother."

He turned back to her with a smile so endearing she lost the battle with tears. "Now, where were we?"

She sniffled.

"Oh darling, please don't cry," he said, his expression crestfallen.

She sniffed again and swiped at her eyes. "I'm not upset, I'm just..." She lost the ability to speak and instead she moved toward him, giving in at last to the urge to touch him.

He moved at the same moment, his arms closing around her and crushing her to his chest. "I just wanted to start over," he murmured against her temple. "I did not mean to upset you."

"I know," she said, shamelessly burrowing into his chest, letting his solid warmth comfort her. "I loved it."

A hand he'd been running over her back stilled. "You did?"

She nodded, pulling her head back far enough to meet his gaze. "I did."

He gave her an adorably crooked smile. "I know there is still much to explain—"

"Yes, and there will be time for all that," she said. "We have time."

"We do?" he asked, hope etched his voice and softened his harsh features.

Her voice was still annoyingly watery, but there was nothing for it. She'd never been so overcome with emotions in all her life. Because today, this evening...she knew.

She knew without a doubt that what mattered most between them was real. He *was* the man she'd fallen in love with. Just...with a different name.

"Does that mean..." He started slowly. "Lottie, does that mean that you believe I did not intend to trick you?"

She nodded. "I know you didn't. Because I've also realized something during that pantomime just now."

He cocked one eyebrow, his eyes already dancing with laughter.

"I realized that you are not a terribly good actor," she said, twining her arms up and around his neck to soften the blow.

"I'm not?" He widened his eyes with mock offense and she burst out laughing.

"Truly terrible," she said with a grin. "But that means that I know now that the most real moments between us... They were not feigned nor trickery."

His gaze darkened, his expression growing serious and tender. "Indeed, they were not. I'm not sure I've ever in my life experienced more honesty than in talking to you and dancing with you..." His lips dropped to hers in a light brush of a kiss. "Kissing you."

Her knees were weak and her body flooded with warmth. "Truly?"

His breath fanned over her lips, making her belly clench with delicious anticipation. "I know it seems odd," he said. "But I think that was the reason I found it so difficult to tell you the truth." He drew in a deep breath. "I meant to. I wanted to. But I was so afraid of losing that connection. Of having you look at me differently."

She nodded in understanding, her throat too choked with emotions to speak.

But fortunately, he did not seem to require speech from her. He dipped his head and grazed his lips over hers again.

She trembled, grateful for the hard crush of his arms around her to hold her upright.

When he kissed her again, harder and yet somehow even more tender, she melted in his arms completely. Her head tipped back, silently asking for more, trusting him to guide her in this new exploration.

"Lottie, my love," he whispered against her lips. "I would never knowingly hurt you. I promise you this."

Her eyelids fluttered open at the earnestness in his gaze. "I believe you."

He groaned as he crushed her to him, his kiss telling her better than words how he'd missed her. How he longed for her.

Their blissful kiss was broken by the sound of dinner being called and then a light tap on the door.

"That will be Mary," he said, his voice gruff as he lovingly stroked her cheek.

She smiled. "So you convinced Mary to be your accomplice, did you?"

He chuckled. "If it makes you feel better, she promised to

end my life if this ended badly." He arched a brow. "You are not angry with her, are you?"

She shook her head. "How could I be? I'm so grateful we had a chance to meet. Again. Officially," she added teasingly.

His grin was so boyish and sweet it made her heart flip.

This was the man she'd come to know.

Her Lord Paul.

No, her Lord Thomas.

Or perhaps just Thomas now.

No. Even better. *Her* Thomas.

She slipped her hand into the crook of his elbow as he led her back toward the dining room.

Now his name hardly mattered.

For now...he was her one true love.

CHAPTER SIXTEEN

Thomas couldn't stop staring at his bride-to-be. She truly was a vision, especially when playing charades.

"If you keep staring like that, everyone will know that you've gone and fallen in love with your fiancée," Paul muttered beside him.

Thomas grinned. "Would that be so bad?"

Just then, Charlotte glanced over and her gaze caught his. Her eyes danced with mischief behind her spectacles and a smile teased her lips.

"It's embarrassing," Paul grumbled.

Thomas supposed that perhaps it was. Or rather, it would be when they rejoined society. Here and now at this intimate house party surrounded mostly by their friends, it was rather idyllic.

"Just look at her," Paul muttered beside him as he too glanced over at Charlotte and Mary, whispering together before the fire. "She's just plain wicked, I tell you. She's up to no good."

Thomas chuckled. He was referring to Mary, of that Thomas was certain.

"What has she done now?" Thomas asked, his gaze still stuck on Charlotte, his mind already conjuring how he might steal her away for another private moment.

"It's not what she's done, it's what she's planning to do," Paul said.

Thomas turned to his friend. "She's planning for a game of charades."

"Precisely." Paul huffed, irritation tugging his normal smile into a grimace. "She's too clever for her own good, that one."

Thomas looked away with a shake of his head. He'd given up on speaking sense where Mary was concerned. As childhood acquaintances, Paul and Mary seemed to have made up their minds about one another, and heaven help anyone who tried to intervene.

When he could abide this separation no longer, Thomas shifted, ready to walk away. "If you'll excuse me. I believe Miss Charlotte might like to see our music room."

"Is that so?" Paul's voice was tinged with disbelief. "Wait." He set a hand on Thomas's arm. "Don't leave me here alone with her."

Thomas gave an exasperated huff. "You're hardly alone."

Not in the most practical of senses, at least. Though Miss Lydia's presence was often forgotten. The poor timid creature seemed happiest when she was tucked alone in a corner with a book rather than a part of the conversation around her.

Miss Farthington had been taken in by his mother and aunt, so while she occasionally spent time with her charges, she was most often dragged along with his mother's crowd.

Meanwhile, he and Charlotte had found every excuse to slip away together whenever it was allowed.

Indeed, as they were engaged, it was usually encouraged.

Well, by all except for Paul and Mary.

"We won't be long," Thomas said. "Perhaps you can find a way to make Lydia participate in charades while we're gone."

Paul muttered something about being named for a saint but not being a miracle worker as Thomas headed off to claim his bride. "Would you care to take a walk with me, Miss Charlotte?"

She beamed up at him. "I should love to."

She slid her gloved fingers into his and fell into step beside him. His heart thudded loudly as it always did when she drew near. He'd come to think of it as his heart greeting hers.

Foolish? Perhaps. But Charlotte had claimed it to be the most romantic sentiment she'd ever heard when he'd told her.

She'd also rewarded him with a kiss that had filled his days and nights with wanting. Truthfully, he hadn't stopped wanting her since the moment they'd first met.

There was a connection between them that could not be denied. And now, fortunately, there was no reason to.

"Where are we going?" she asked as they strode slowly down a hallway.

He shrugged. "The library. The music room. The atrium. The choice is yours, my lady, I merely wished for the pleasure of your company."

She sighed. "I'm grateful you sought me out." She caught her lip between her teeth as she peeked up at him. "Is it wrong to admit that I've missed you today?"

He grinned. They'd been in one another's company ever since breakfast. But he knew precisely what she meant. "Not at all," he said. "I could not abide another moment standing so far apart from you."

She sighed sweetly again, her head resting lightly against

his shoulder. "I do love that we've had this time to truly get to know one another."

He nodded. He felt the same. It had been a relief to spend such time with her without lies and misunderstandings hanging overhead.

For the first time in his life, he never failed for conversation. Not with her, at least. They could not seem to stop talking when they were together. Their interest in one another was endless. And the more he knew her, the more he loved her.

And the feeling was mutual, he believed.

They shared an understanding that was so much more than anything he'd ever dared imagine.

She was not just his bride-to-be, nor even merely the woman he felt attracted to. She was his friend. His dearest friend as well as the woman who owned his heart.

"Thomas?"

"Yes, my love?"

She glanced up at him shyly. "I have been enjoying this time we've had together. But if I'm being honest, I..." She bit her lip. "I find I'm growing impatient to marry."

They'd just entered the empty atrium, and he growled low in his throat as he spun to face her, his hands coming to her waist as he moved until her back was pressed to the wall. "Oh, my darling. I find I cannot tolerate having you so close and yet not having you as my own."

She sank into him, her lips parted and her eyes dazed. "But I *am* yours. You know that."

He was still smiling as his lips claimed hers.

She had given him her heart, yes. But he was ready for more. He wanted no barriers between them. No other people around them with their expectations and demands. He could hardly wait for the day when this relationship was solely about them.

With that thought, he pulled back with a sigh.

"What is it?" she asked.

He sighed as he pulled a letter from his pocket. "The timing of our nuptials is what I wanted to discuss with you today."

She arched a brow as she eyed the missive. "A letter?" Her lips pursed. "From your father or mine?"

He huffed with amusement. "Clever girl," he murmured.

She grinned.

"This one was from *my* father." He eyed it with displeasure, even though, in the end, he actually shared his father's interests for once. "He and your father are angling for a quick wedding."

She huffed. "Of course, they are." She planted her hands on her hips. "Am I extraordinarily contrary if I hate that I want the same as them?"

He chuckled. "I was just thinking the same."

While his mother and Miss Farthington were well aware of the happy state of their new relationship, the letters they'd been receiving from her parents and his father made it clear that they worried one or both of them would cry off during this house party.

They'd all but ordered them to return twice now to get the wedding plans underway. Truly, their time was running out either way. The Season was set to begin soon and Miss Farthington had a duty to her other charges as well.

They'd been sent to the School of Charm for a reason, and that reason was not to stay hidden away at a country manor while the rest of society enjoyed the Season.

"I suppose we must go back," Charlotte said. With a courageous smile, she added, "Fortunately the sooner we return the sooner we can be wed and the sooner we will be married."

"And away from our parents," he added.

She nodded. "Indeed. We are almost to the best part of the story, Thomas. And I for one am impatient to get there."

He chuckled. "Did you just compare our marriage to a good book, Lottie?"

She laughed. "It seemed fitting."

He pulled her into his arms and held her tight. How had he gotten so lucky?

She rested her head against his chest with a sweet sigh.

"Lottie," he said slowly as his mind went back to this most recent missive and a plan began to form.

"Thomas," she said, a mischievous grin on her lips as she tilted her head back to look up at him. "I know that tone."

He smiled. "I was just thinking..."

"Scheming, more like," she shot back.

"I told you why our fathers are in such a rush to see us wed..."

She nodded. They'd had that conversation on one of her first days here at the manor.

In the aftermath of his fight with his father, Thomas hadn't just argued with his father, he'd demanded answers.

The answers were hardly heartwarming. As suspected, this marriage wasn't at all about their happiness or comfort, but about money and political power.

Money was what his father needed, and in exchange he had the influence that her father desired.

And so they'd bought and sold their children to seal the deal.

Not unusual and not unfair. And truly, now that they knew they loved each other, it had all worked out quite splendidly.

But even so, neither he nor Lottie enjoyed feeling like pawns.

And he was beginning to think it time that they found some power of their own.

"What are you thinking?" Charlotte asked.

"Just that our fathers had hoped to forge an alliance with our marriage. They need us." He gripped her hands. "They need this."

She nodded, her lips twitching with mirth as her hands squeezed his. "They'd set out to create this amalgamation." Her eyes danced with laughter now. "But I suspect they did not count on this."

He laughed as he tugged on her hands until she was once more settled within his arms. "No, indeed. And that is my point precisely. They are as of yet unaware of our feelings for one another."

Indeed, he'd asked his mother pointedly not to share any confidences with his father. Not to be secretive but out of respect for their burgeoning feelings.

"Our Frankenstein fathers do not yet realize they've created something that has taken on a life of its own," she said with a laugh.

He leaned down and brushed his nose against hers. "My dear, are you calling my love for you a monster?"

Her head fell back with a laugh, the sweetest sound in the world. "Of course not. But it does have a certain dramatic flair, does it not?" She arched a brow teasingly. "This thing between us has certainly taken on a life of its own."

He nodded, still chuckling. "And together we certainly are a force to be reckoned with."

Her eyes narrowed in thought. "What do you propose?"

His lips twitched upward in a secretive smile. "Only that we ensure our own happiness as well as theirs."

Her brows arched. "I should think marrying one another will ensure that."

"Yes," he agreed quickly. "But I would like our actual marriage to be conducted on our terms, with autonomy from our families and freedom from their expectations."

Her eyes fairly glowed with delight. "Oh, I like the sound of that."

"It is settled then." He grinned, leaning down to kiss the tip of her nose. "We shall marry, and quickly—but not until we've settled our terms with our families."

She nodded, a dazed smile on her lips. "I do so love it when you talk grand plans and mischievous schemes."

He grinned. "And I love that you are going to be mine. Forever and always."

She sighed as his lips brushed over hers. "Oh yes, I love that most of all."

The conversation ended as his lips met hers once more and clung. It was a slow kiss. A sweet kiss.

A kiss that promised their own happily ever after.

EPILOGUE

Two months later...

THE RUINS of the Roman empire were not half so fascinating as her new husband's perfect profile.

"Stay still," Charlotte tsked as she sketched.

He did not stay still. In fact, her dashing husband broke his pose entirely to lean over and kiss her cheek.

"Thomas!" she laughed.

"I'm sorry, my love, it could not be helped." He did not look apologetic. Not in the least.

Not that she minded. Putting away her materials, she turned to see her husband lounging again, though with a far more relaxed position than before when he'd been posing for her artwork.

"Is it everything you'd hoped?" she asked.

He nodded, his expression distant and a now-familiar smile softening his features as he gazed at the sites of

Pompeii spread before him. "It is better." He reached for her hand and squeezed it. "Because I am here with you."

"I feel the same," she said softly.

As if it needed to be stated. They had not been married for long, but each day had been a gift. Better than any future she'd dare dream for herself.

Thomas had been true to his word, using that stern demeanor he'd learned so well from his father to negotiate with the earl and the viscount until a new contract had been drafted.

One that had met his approval...and hers.

Of course, they had not known that she'd had a say in the matter. Still didn't, she supposed. But it mattered not what their families thought of their swift marriage and rapidly planned travels shortly after.

Out of society and away from the *ton,* Charlotte discovered more freedom than she'd ever imagined. Thomas too. Looking at him now with that smile on his face and the relaxed posture, it was difficult to imagine how she'd ever thought his features forbidding or his voice stern.

He was thoughtful and kind, humorous and clever. Most of all he shared her love of romance and adventure.

And mischief.

Her new husband most certainly enjoyed his mischief.

They nibbled on some bread and cheese, relaxing under the hot, setting sun as they reveled in the views and the activity going on about them.

"Oh, I nearly forgot," Thomas said. "The manager of the hotel gave me some correspondence as we were leaving for today's jaunt."

He pulled out a stack of letters that had finally caught up with them. The top letter he handed to Charlotte.

She grinned at the familiar handwriting. "Aunt Ida!" She

scanned the letter briefly, excitement making her pulse flutter as she reached for Thomas's hand. "She wishes for us to join her in Greece. And from there she'd like for us to accompany her to Egypt."

Her heart nearly flew out of her chest at the excitement in Thomas's expression. "That would be fascinating."

She grinned. "I think so too."

He leaned over to kiss her, as if he couldn't restrain himself for one more moment.

This time she forgot about the crowds, forgot entirely that they might be causing a scandal.

She kissed him back with all the happiness that was in her heart.

When at last they pulled apart, Thomas gestured to the rest of the letters. He handed one to her while he took the other.

"Mine is from Mary," she said with a smile.

"And mine is from Paul." He turned to her and gave her a knowing wink.

"Let's see what they say," she said. When she was done reading, her mouth gaped open in shock. "I cannot believe it."

Thomas was staring at his letter with a similar expression. "Paul says..." He turned to her. "Can it be?"

"They're married?" she exclaimed.

"But how? Why?" he started.

She shook her head. Mary had been dreadfully sparse with the details. "I don't know but there must be a story there."

"Oh yes, there must," he said in a low ominous tone. Then amusement flickered in his eyes. "And I'd wager it's a good one."

* * *

THANK YOU FOR READING! Up next, Mary and Paul bicker their way to true love in *The Misguided Miss Mary,* available now at https://maggiedallenbooks.com

ABOUT THE AUTHOR

Maggie Dallen writes adult and young adult romantic comedies in a range of genres. An unapologetic addict of all things romance, she loves to connect with fellow avid readers on Facebook, Twitter or at www.maggiedallen.com. For a FREE sweet regency romance, sign up for her monthly newsletter at http://eepurl.com/bFEVsL

ND - #0386 - 270525 - C0 - 203/127/10 - PB - 9781736574195 - Matt Lamination